LOUIS XXX

Georges Bataille

ALSO BY STUART KENDALL

CRITICISM
Georges Bataille
The Ends of Art and Design

TRANSLATION
Gilgamesh
Georges Bataille, *The Cradle of Humanity: Prehistoric Art and Culture*
Georges Bataille, *Guilty*
Georges Bataille, *The Unfinished System of Nonknowledge*
Jean Baudrillard, *Utopia Deferred*
Maurice Blanchot, *Lautréamont and Sade*
Guy Debord, *Correspondence*
Paul Éluard, *Love, Poetry*

EDITED
Terrence Malick: Film and Philosophy (with Thomas Deane Tucker)

Georges Bataille

Louis XXX

The Little One *and* The Tomb of Louis XXX

Translated and with Commentary by
Stuart Kendall

EQUUS

Copyright © Georges Bataille, 1936, 1971, 2004.
Translation and Commentary © Stuart Kendall, 2013.
Georges Bataille, "Le Petit," *Oeuvres complètes* tome 3 (Paris: Gallimard, 1971); "La Tombe de Louis XXX," *Oeuvres complètes* tome 4 (Paris: Gallimard, 1971).

ISBN 978-0-9571213-5-5

Equus Press
Birkbeck College (William Rowe), 43 Gordon Square, London, WC1 H0PD, United Kingdom

Typeset: lazarus
Cover design: Interior Ministry
Printed in the Czech Republic by PB Tisk

All rights reserved.

Composed in 10pt Janson, erroneously named for the seventeenth-century Dutch punch-cutter Anton Janson, designed by Miklós Tótfalusi Kis c.1685.

Contents

Preface

Georges Bataille never planned to publish the texts contained in this book together. As I explain in the postface, both of these texts have their origins in the fall of 1942, during months when Bataille was also writing *Guilty*, *The Accursed Share*, *The Oresteia* and other works. *The Little One* was completed and published under the signature of Louis Trente the following June, in a small edition meant for private circulation. Thereafter, unlike most of Bataille's other published shorter works, this one was never reprinted. After its initial publication, *The Little One* was denied, effaced, or buried within his oeuvre.

The Tomb of Louis XXX was prepared for publication at least as early as 1947, but, for unknown reasons, Bataille abandoned the project and the text took its place alongside many other completed or nearly completed texts that the perfectionistic, careless, or perhaps simply distracted author did not see through to publication. While Bataille did abandon much of his writing – more than one quarter of his *Oeuvres Complètes* consists of materials he did not publish at all; another quarter consists of articles and short pieces he neglected to collect – he also demonstrated an obsessive or quasi-obsessive interest in his texts: he repeatedly republished his writings, often reworking them, rewriting or reorganizing them or supplementing them with additional prefaces and addenda.

But what of these two texts? They stand apart in an oeuvre that stands apart. Bringing them together here will not change that, but hopefully it will permit us to glimpse the source of the laceration that binds them together under one name.

Louis Trente

The Little One

Evil

… a festival for myself alone, at which, no longer able to maintain it, I break the tie that binds me to others.[i] I tolerate no fidelity to this bond. No one loves who is not led to break it. The complete act of love would be to throw myself naked into the night, in the street, not for a prostitute but in order to live an *impossible* by myself in so sure a silence. I would do the inadmissible there, not something that I could describe with some insignificant vulgarity that you wouldn't think about. I could defecate, lie down there and cry. I would shame even those who flatter themselves by assuming they understand me — those who imagine that I'm not vulgar. I want neither to delight nor disgust myself but…

Large eyes wide open, looking at the sky, the stars, in a state of innocence.

To be a woman overcome, stripped, white eyes. Dream of absence, not of pleasure. Absent, she is nevertheless the evil that is greedy for delight, in evil, the need to deny the order without which one could not live.

Men misunderstand each other in the good and love each other in evil. The good is hypocrisy. Evil is love. Innocence is the love of sin.

When it arouses interest, evil is a good for the evil-doer. Authentic evil is disinterested.

In its intimacy, its gentleness, its disinterestedness, society rests on evil: it is like the night, made of anguish.

To banish a part of man and deprive it of life, to impose on everyone, with a sick incomprehension, the exile of a part of themselves…

Gripped by shame, to deny the horror that one has beneath oneself, to absorb oneself foolishly in the dream of a man who would be this lie, obfuscation of what he has beneath him…

One day, a naked girl in my arms, my fingers caressing the crack of her arse. I spoke to her gently of the "little one." She understood. I didn't know that they sometimes referred to It in this way in brothels.

If I evoke a childhood, soiled and swallowed up, condemned to dissimulation, it is the gentlest voice in me that cries: I myself am the "little one," I only have a hidden place.

One poorly imagines the tenderness of the little one condemned to a bad conscience. One would cry with me, supposing it bound, capable only of horror, and this with a suspicious and tender courage.

My head cannot explode, is but a wrist twisted... by whom? "What I know" continues on the inside, turning there. Not knowing what to do or how to do it. Sleep? I will have to be awoken. To speak of a voice beneath centuries of silence. There is no good. If there is no good, there is nothing.

This God who animates us under swarming clouds is mad. I know it, I am this God.

Miserere Dei...
To divine me would be... what anguish! Divine anguish: no responsibility, no task to fulfil, no good to realise. Everything is consummated, there is no longer anything but the radiation of this agony.[ii]

The "little one": radiation of agony, of death, radiation of a dead star, burst in the sky announcing death — beauty of the day at twilight under low clouds, sudden downpour chased by the wind.

I sleep and dream. Naked beside a girl I drew into a debauchery of lacerating joys: the kind I know, now, outside any access, of which a painful dream is the conscience. My dream responds to the state of the dead star where I am, the distant dead star still shines, loses its rays in a living immensity: I recall myself dead…

What stupidity my story would be without the suffocating filthiness of the "little one," again yesterday I was able to get in bed, to cry, delirious with shame. How to cry out the horror that this was yesterday?

I come while laughing at the misfortune to come. I don't have the strength to laugh at that misfortune, others will laugh at it, I urge them to. It would be despicable not to laugh at my death. I deserve it.[iii]

The depth of sufferings, wherein one doesn't imagine any desirable way out, wherein the possible always has a lifeless face.[iv]

Neurosis: nostalgia for God's anguish.

How comical it is to return things and explain my conduct with psychiatry: to do it with, like me, a "little one."[v] Neurosis is made responsible, one eludes the insoluble enigma, a presence on the ground awaiting what? Unable to respond, one feigns having already answered, the neurosis alone opposed to the success that is certain without it! The contrary made evident: a practical joker's success alone opposed to the feeling of the agonizing enigma — neurosis is the timorous apprehension of a depth of the impossible to which one gives some accidental cause, instead of accepting its unavoidable nature. The impossible is the depth of being... Neurosis implicates it in a circumstance when it isn't there, in which the normal human is right to call it sick, but it comes up from the depth of being to which the normal remain strangers (except in laughter, vice, poetry, devotion, war...).

To write bare-stomached and bare-arsed, to write and to find the innocence that I have pulling away my shorts.

Cool in the humid obscurity of a corridor, the insinuated hand is the hand of evil.[vi]

Neurosis wastes a possibility of happiness, what happens, or what little is necessary of it, of each possible happiness. One incriminates sickness, wickedness, one pushes away an expiring truth, uttered with great pain, that wants to make itself heard and no longer has the strength to do so: the impossible in the depth of things exhales an unappeasable agitation, one submits to its law but questions, one clings to the fiction with a guilty, suppressible strength, without which one would take pleasure in happiness.

Man is thirsty for evil, for the guilty element, but does not dare (or is unable) to give his soul to it, takes the oblique course, neurosis, laughter, etc.

To say: "God is evil" is by no means what one imagines. This is a tender truth, of friendship with death, a slipping into the void, into absence.

But God is not evil: cannot be evil, not being good. I attain God in evil, beings unite, know exorbitant love in evil. I don't know an innocent God but a guilty one, his innocence is the same thing as the evil in me, as the velvet sex of a young girl, so angelic was she, the same as my gland.

God is worse or more distant than evil, is the innocence of evil.

The weak: "There is no evil, everything is pure and science offers proof of this." But the strong: "Evil is the impossible existing in the depth of things, that indirectly reveals vices, crimes, wars."

Obliquely, consciousness of the impossible at the depth of things unites man. The girl and the boy are confounded in an unnameable discovery (crevices of filth). The human type is united in the memory of its crime: God translated into justice, condemned, put to death.

The two most common images: the cross, the cock.[vii]

I throw myself directly into the impossible: delivered to others — united intimately — writing bare-stomached. Like a revolted girl, white eyes, without individual existence.

Remorse is within me, the past gnaws at me. That which God does not endure, the past, the irreparable! God not being the horror of memory (but what do I have to say about him other than cries? …).

Innocent? Guilty? Imbecile? But the past, but the irreparable… and so old, a filthiness that one cannot clean, on which one must live.

In pure evil, by no means does one want the good of man, but one cannot forget that the good of man is not the good, that his evil is not evil. Shattered categories: I can want evil itself, to the point of affirming it in a pure gift of love from myself to others. I wouldn't want this evil if my surviving sense of the good didn't make me feel remorse, did not obligate me to plunge myself into evil.

How is this evil the evil, since in the end it is the good of man? This evil excludes appeasement, dispels the assurance of happiness: it sacrifices life, consumes it dangerously, devotes it to the sacred, to anguish.

If I destroy in order to augment my power — or my personal enjoyment — I am in part on the side of good, this is useful in sum. This is what one commonly calls evil: a disorder from the perspective of a different order. One must always imagine, nevertheless, that in enjoyment, or power, the evil was wanted for itself: enjoyment, power, might have only been a means.

The demand of evil is so profound, so harsh, that my momentary lucidity and peace are contrary to it. Writing, very quickly I cannot respond to so complete a demand: to write engages partially in the path of the good.

I am delighted by my past debaucheries. I recollect them at length in scabrous detail. I am most often pleased. The savour of an arse, a mouth, breasts, especially the sensation of nudity: one girl infinitely more naked than another, miraculously naked, sometimes in her stockings, her belt, a jacket, another time completely bare, naked feet. But always the crack of her arse open to my eyes, to my hands... — sometimes to other eyes... At that point the girl's mouth is deep, deeper than the night, than the sky, by reason of her naked arse. An intimate caress in the crack and the mouth is afraid, becomes acrid, divine... Other insipid girls, with a stomach, an arse, hardly as naked as an apple... But real nudity, acrid, maternal, silently white and faecal as a barn, this bacchant truth, glands in the legs and lips, is the ultimate truth of the earth, at once pithiatic[viii] and wanting to remain in shadow, accepting condemnation as the gods always do, only ever opening dying eyes.

No truth more secret, or more suspiciously chaste: it must be for it to be mistaken under the mask of vice (vulgar, interested).

The erotic sky opened: coincidence of festival music (lost frenzy) and the silence of death.

The pure erotic:
the crater,
the impossible, it rises in the throat, has the scent of blood.

Debauchery: divine impossible under a resolutely vulgar mask. God alone is masked here, not the impossible. At church, God alone is a completed mask of the impossible. The good God, sugary cowardice, deicide, masks not only the impossible but God.

The refinement of God in vice: to give himself, under a suave mask, to the devotee, to die beribboned by the embarrassments of a sexagenarian virgin.

As at the brothel.
God has the "choice."

God: "human" possibility without the circumstantial limitations in which man fails.

On the edge of a field of beets, at twilight, under a black cloud sprawling from the magisterial stratums in a "white of the eyes" sky, the "little one" crouching, bare-arsed, makes the divine limits recoil. His thought looking for itself in the mazes of the sky, he is lost and like a dog — his tail made subtle by the devil — would search for it (his tail: the knowledge that he has of the world), he turns — comically, sadly, what you will — around himself, without escape, catching nothing.

God does not endure an instant of thought; this is why he cannot exist.

Who will divine God?
Who will know knowing nothing?
Who will lose his way?

[23]

Who interrogating death will know himself when dead?

I am speaking of this in order to translate a state of terror.

In place of God…

there is
only
the impossible,
and not God.

Lacerations, their echoes reverberate in the sky. It is no less empty of me (the sky), foreign to my head in that it escapes losing its head.

Comical incident.

In this moment I am living at… with peasants.

In the middle of the night, someone pounds heavily on the door to my room.

A crime has just been committed: the circumstances suggested that I be accused. The policemen were arresting me.

I sat up in bed and cried out:

"Who is there?"

A wedding party called out to me:

"Hey, in there, the groom!"

"Ah, but no," I said, "it's not me."

The wedding party burst out laughing (a little annoyed).

They had the wrong room. I came home late and I had forgotten that, on this particular night, my hosts were lodging a couple of newlyweds.

In the same instant, I dreamed the crime and the policemen, the way Maury dreamt of the guillotine.[ix]

At dawn, the wedding party came back, the accordion sang: "All goes very well, Madame la marquise…" and in the room next door at the top of their lungs: "Long live the Bride!" After a rumpus, an indecent round of young girls around the wedding bed, everyone left, the couple dressed in a no time. I went to the window and, gaily, designated to the wedding party the head of the counterfeit groom, of the counterfeit guilt. November weather, mud, fog in the village street.

I thought: "None of them ask themselves even a little question." Then: "No imaginable question, at least one of them is not committing a crime." I imagine philosophy (Wolf, Comte, and swarms of professors[x]) like a village wedding: no questions and, only, with a headache, Kierkegaard[xi] interrogates (offers himself some responses, interrogates anyway).

And now: more the shadow of a response. The empty sky, last night, on the field of beets, suspicious and magisterial, this sordid and grey morning, lid lowered on the village buffoonery. Nothing but me, the "little one," in my room, among photographic enlargements and pious images, impossible, and all alone. It has been raining endlessly for a week.

Memory, the mechanism of sufferings, of the limits of a being (in this of the joys bound to the suffering, to the limits, to the isolation of being), remaining entirely prey to the future. If I give up my anxiety about a time to come, an intoxication with life follows remorse, drunkenness in one form or another. In the same way my concern for the future, if it's real, if it's anxious, differs in no way from remorse: one isn't afraid of suffering but of being guilty. In other words, my remorse is the remorse that I will have. Remorse begins because of the present, the time that I must spend in such a way that a "guilty" sentence doesn't surprise me tomorrow. And in the irreparable — "it's too late!" — the situation is changed only in that one can no longer do anything, the "guilt" is still a category of time to come: when the sentence is pronounced, when it falls, it frees one from remorse! Remorse is a threat, a threat of misfortune, a threat of remorse. The accomplished threat, the remorse *there*, it is still in the memory-future mechanism that spreads out the suffering. It is a property of suffering to chase being from the present: the remorse that persists in misfortune is always a threat in the mechanism in which memory persists.

In death, no longer any anxiety over the future: one does oneself in. The same in God. At least, consumed with ferocity, man does not threaten a dying person with survival, does not put God in the service of the servitude he wants for himself.

The human condition given by the mechanism of a memory functioning for the future, a man, from that moment, describes the divine condition. At first glance, one sees this as a power of being in place of the limit that it is (of servitude). To give God anxiety, memory, is the extremity of our powerlessness — execrable cruelty turned back against ourselves.

The only possible time? Here it would be like the elephant who according to some would carry the earth? … where the brain falls to the pavement like a glass of milk and shatter.

God is by no means evil, but in the debate between good and evil, man glimpses the abyss. The murder of Jesus, the infamy, the impossible in this murder describes God so truthfully that while dreaming about it my nostrils flare. How will I guess what fate will make of me in such instants? I no longer worry about it: all of the sudden, I see myself as God's guinea pig but God in his infinity, is blind while sight is my infirmity.

Have pity on me, I might be blind. And why would I survive? Why not be God, this corpse? … I don't know. I am writing in bed at three in the morning, outside, it's pouring; I should go out naked in the rain, blindfolded, to die eating the earth.

I do not know what this means: if this is not destroyed, I offer more ignorance to whoever really wants it (imagine the psychiatrist who would know it? Is there anything more stupid?). One single thing: writing, towards the end, I understood that I was nostalgic for dying, for making myself a stranger to laws, free like a dying man, who does himself in and has nothing more to see in the time to come.

What tenderness now…
  O how blind I am!
  I survive the state of a soft voice saying (it's always night, it's always raining): "to live like a dying man!" I don't know why my tenderness imagines robust peasant bodies and men who already know hard skulls, adhering to the dead eyes of the blind. How many such people, dying in front of others, have respect for this life that is completed in them, how many hide themselves, that they need hardly any space. Not to scandalise, to give the earth — at least in the night — the "freedom" of the dying.

First Epilogue

Not to remain God nor that for which man thirsts. To follow a cursed path…

To laugh, happy and cursed, ignoring, ingenuous.

Going to the depths of being, it is possible for me, with a concept, to "tempt God," to draw him out of the "impossible."
Going to the depths of being, I introduce untenable concepts, the most audacious ones that can be made.

I have no complaisance in evil.

Nothing should be strained, drawn to defeat. A Laocoönian combat, a rat fight in a cellar for the human possible and impossible. Who will know what kindness sustains me, what lover's insolence, what sudden decisive fury?

My kindness: anguish and love, tenderness and tears are wed. Good and evil are wed.

W.C.

Preface to the *Story of the Eye*

A year before *Story of the Eye*, I wrote a book entitled *W.C.*: a little book but crazy enough. *W.C.* was as lugubrious as *Story of the Eye* is juvenile. The manuscript of *W.C.* was burned,[xii] this isn't too bad given my present sadness: this book was a cry of horror (horror of myself, not of my debauchery, but of the philosopher's head wherein since... how sad it is!) I remain content, on the contrary, with the fulminating joy of the *Eye*: nothing can efface it. Unequalled joy, what limits a naive extravagance, remains beyond anguish. In it anguish reveals its meaning.

A drawing in *W.C.* showed an eye: that of the scaffold. Solitary, solar, bristling with lashes, it opened in the lunette of the guillotine. This drawing's name was the *eternal return*, and this horrible machine was its gateway. Extending to the horizon, the path of eternity passed there. A parodic verse, heard in a sketch at the Concert Mayol, had given me the inscription:
— *God, the body's blood is sad in the depths of sound.*[xiii]

There is another reminiscence of *W.C.* in *Story of the Eye*, which from the title page inscribed the following under the worst of signs. The name Lord Auch recalls the habit of a friend of mine: when irritated, he said, "aux chiottes!" [*to the shithouse*], or even shortened this to say "aux ch.'" Lord in English means God (in holy writings): Lord Auch is God relieving himself. The liveliness of this story forbids weighing it down; each being leaves transfigured from such a place: that God sinks here rejuvenates the heavens.

To be God, naked, solar in the rainy night, in a field: red, divinely scattering shit with the majesty of a storm, face grimacing, torn apart, to be in tears IMPOSSIBLE: who knew, before me, what majesty was?

The *eye of conscience* and the *wood of justice* incarnate the eternal return, is there a more desperate image of remorse?

I gave the author of *W.C.* the pseudonym Troppmann.[xiv]

I jerked off naked in the night, beside my mother's corpse[xv] (some people have doubted it, reading *Coincidences*: doesn't this have the fictional character of the tale? Like the *Preface*, *Coincidences* has a literal exactness: many people from the village R. could confirm its substance; just the same, some of my friends have read *W.C.*).[xvi]

What struck me more: seeing my father shit a great number of times. Climbing down from his blind paralytic's bed (my father was both blind and paralytic). He climbed down with difficulty (I helped him), he sat down on the pot, in his nightshirt and often topped with a cotton nightcap (he had a pointed grey beard, ill kept, a large eagle-nose and immense hollow eyes, fixed on the void). At times, "lightning sharp pains" tore the cry of a beast from him, sticking out his bent leg that he hugged in his arms in vain.

My father having conceived me when blind (absolutely blind), I cannot tear out my eyes like Oedipus.

Like Oedipus I have solved the riddle: no one has divined it more deeply than I.

6 November 1915, in a bombarded town, four or five kilometres from the German lines, my father died abandoned.

My mother and I abandoned him to the German advance in August 1914.

We left him to the housekeeper.

The Germans occupied the town, then evacuated it. It was then a question of returning: my mother, unable to stand the idea, went mad. Toward the end of the year, my mother recovered: she refused to let me return to N.[xvii] We rarely received letters from my father, he went off the rails with difficulty. When we learned he was dying, my mother agreed to leave with me. He died a few days before we arrived, asking for his children: we found a sealed coffin in the room.

When my father went mad (one year before the war) after a hallucinating night, my mother sent me to post a telegram.[xviii] I recall having been seized by a horrible pride on that road. Misery overwhelmed me, an inner irony responded: "so much horror predestines you!" Some months earlier, one beautiful December morning, I warned my parents, who were beside themselves, that I would never again set foot in a school. No amount of anger would change my resolution: I lived alone, going out only rarely and by way of the fields, avoiding the centre of town where I might run into friends.

My father, an irreligious man, died refusing a priest. During puberty, I was irreligious myself (my mother was indifferent). But I went to see a priest in August 1914 and, until 1920, went rarely a week without confessing my sins! At 20, I changed again, ceasing to believe in anything other than chance. My piety was but an attempt at evasion: I wanted to elude my destiny at all costs; I abandoned my father. Today, I know myself "blind" without measure, man "abandoned" on the globe like my father at N. No one on earth or in the heavens cared about my father's agony. At the same time, I believe, as always, he faced it. What "horrible pride," at times, in dad's blind smile!

Absence of Remorse[xix]

I have shit in my eyes
I have shit in my heart
God flows away
laughs
radiant
intoxicates the sky
the sky sings at the top of its lungs the sky
sings
the thunder sings
solar lightning sings
dry eyes
broken silence of shit in the heart

If a joyous gland engendered the universe, it would make it as it is: one should, in the transparency of the sky, of blood, of cries, of stink.

God is not a priest but a gland: papa is a gland.

my crack is a friend
in the eyes of fine wine
and my crime is a friend
to delicate brandied lips

I shake myself from reason
wipe myself from the apple

A Little Later

To write is to research chance.[xx]

Chance animates the smallest parts of the universe: the scintillation of the stars is its power, a flower in the field its incantation.

The warmth of life had left me, desire found no objects: my hostile fingers, sore, always wove the canvas of chance.

To give chance so unhappy an anguish, I had the feeling of bringing it the missing thread.

Happily, I was played by chance, I was her thing, CHANCE was the sun in the outstretched haze of my misfortune.

I lost it but knowing the secrets of words I maintain the bond of writing between chance and myself.[xxi]

The point of chance is veiled in the sadness of this book. This point would be inaccessible without it.

Georges Bataille

The Tomb of Louis XXX

Dregs
the exhaustion of an odious heart
acrid
the gentle intimacy of vice

the SKY inverted in your eyes.

Tomb of the wind
Tomb of the river

my death falsifies my voice
which only reaches

aching teeth

little flower
little ear you know
the extent to which
I'm afraid of shit.

At night
look at the sky
the crack behind.[xxii]

The wound is fresh
disfiguring
the red stream
the cut hardens

there is no longer any eye
it's me.

The Oratorio

Characters

The Recitant
The Whore. 90 years old, dying (she was adorably beautiful at 20; one day while naked she rendered God the service that, in the *120 Days*, D'Aucourt renders to Duclos.[xxiii])
The Priest, 30 years old.
God, from a stone.

The Recitant names and presents the characters. There is no costume or decor. The scene takes place in the whore's room.

She says:

> To the sewer[xxiv]
> I am the sewer
> Alas!

Herr priest says:

> I am Herr priest
> your little boy
> caress my
> ear
> while dying.
> *O my host*
> *my sewer my mother*
> *I lift you in the sky*

The stone says:

> I am God
> I hit you on the head
> Herr priest
> I kill you
> I am a cunt.[xxv]

The Book

I drink in your laceration
and I spread your naked legs
I open them as a book
wherein I read that which kills
me. [xxvi]

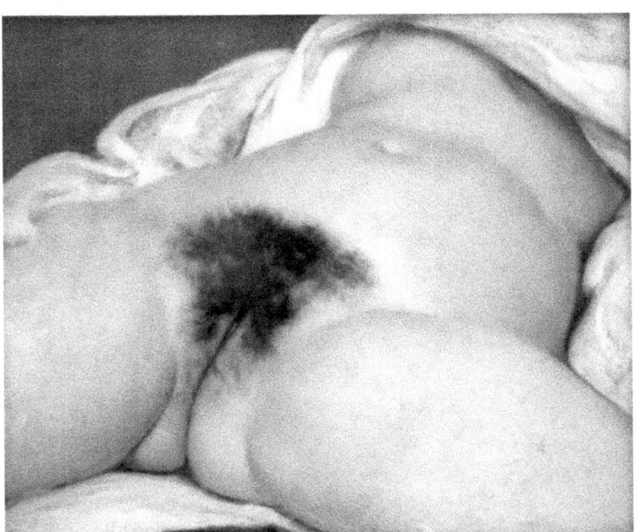

Meditation

... When I first began to meditate, I habitually entered a state of torpor, wherein I suddenly felt myself become an erect penis. The intensity of my conviction rendered it difficult to deny. The previous day I had had the same kind of violent feeling, the feeling that I was a tree and, without being able to oppose the idea, in the darkness, my arms extended themselves as branches. The idea of being — my body, my head — a large hardening penis was so crazy that I felt like laughing. The comical idea even came to me that so hard an erection — the entire body tensed as a hard tail — had no other point than orgasm! Besides, it was impossible to laugh at such a moment: like the torture victim I have a picture of, my eyes were, I think, turned around in their orbits, my head turned around, lips open. In that unexpected state, the memory of this photograph came to my mind without provoking the habitual depression: a rush of horror, of light, brought me from the depths to the heights. Nothing exceeds the feeling inspired in me by torture more.

Since then I avoided these sorts of awful changes (the scandalous element in me is involuntary: it always *overtakes* me). But one year later, in the grip of sexual excitation (that I should have resisted), I ended up naked in my room. I saw myself standing in the most libertine scenes. I entered into a difficult state to describe, near to a nightmare and painful: torpor and exasperation combined. Naked, I went down into the vast, empty house and sat down on the bathroom throne. I hoped that defecation would set me free. I twisted myself red and could have cried: I found myself in my room and greedy for women no less than before. In the end, my body stretched itself, like the preceding year, again the image of torture shattered me. I fell to the earth…

Time passed without suffering seems vain or, if one prefers, awkward, compared to time that ordains unhappiness. Not that profound suffering carries us to some goal and owes some result to this detour! Authentic suffering tells us: "Neither goal nor result justifies my cruelty; in no way were you able to hold onto the weakest hope: I bring only myself, I want you entirely, no conditions." Still one must confess:

"If suffering wasn't what it is, contrary to desire, it would respond to the desire that we have to escape limits. This is why, in its power, everything that is not suffering seems vain."[xxvii]

I imagined that I condemned myself to silence, to an
indefinite suffering, so great that words…

I thought: "How cruel my suffering is, — no one is more talkative than I am!"

These sufferings that make the dead breathe... In advance, death encircles us with an endless silence the way an island is surrounded by water. But the unspeakable is justly there. What importance do words that don't pierce the silence have? Why speak of a "grave moment," when each word is nothing because it doesn't reach beyond words?

I know that I have brought things to the end, or so my
boredom tells me.

The destruction of language isn't my act, what destroys
me has no place in me, as the act of the moment that has
suppressed me (now I'm talking, but in vain).

Are my writings intended for the use of *sovereigns*? If I alienate myself, with a concession made to the values of utility, the moments of horror, being the support of a "sovereign good," I exchange (I sell) the sovereignty that belongs to me as a commodity: so as to no longer be afraid.

But this fear at risk is no less desire than horror: it is anguish (wherein the desire that I have for an object that frightens me (to no longer be) hollows out (enriches) my fright). If I grant reasons to fear, if I said "God," I would alienate a sovereignty that wants the fear of no longer existing to be surmounted in me, I would pass into the service of utility (by a detour, since utility comes from being — God guarantees that it transcends *being* — serving God lowers it before this principle : that *being* remain, that it should be imperishable).

I am unable to doubt death any longer. Further, I am no longer able to desire if not death itself then what death announces: a dawn of death.

Nudity, the urinary crack, the vicinities of shit are to death what the sunrise is to the day. At every moment, the obscenity of the "little death" reminds me of the horror of the "big" one. God saves me no more from my shitty nudity than from rotting in the earth.

The excess of pleasure from a naked girl, prick in her mouth, is for me like a guarantee of definitive night. If I said: "before all else, we must endure," I would have to condemn the girl. But I would renounce my sovereignty from the beginning (on my knees, I would say: "My God!"). Religiosity (to go to the end of life's possibilities, which we can do *together*) has two paths, one servile, the other sovereign. The first is not only immediate loss, but it subordinates all value to the *end*, God himself, to utility (which is to say to being). The second exhausts itself and has no point. It implies:

   — desire, in anguish, carried away by fear;

   — awareness that a sovereign pleasure is a challenge (*happiness*, that makes luck possible) that I bring to death;

   — the idea that the night wherein I fall cannot be compensated anywhere, in any way; without this I would be subordinate to the "possible," which would compensate for it, in place of being abandoned (as I am) to my sovereignty (to the night which will never see the dawn).[xxviii]

Larvatus Prodeo

I is an other.
Arthur Rimbaud,
Letter to Paul Demeny

Every philosophy also *conceals* a
philosophy; every opinion is also a
hideout, every word also a mask.
Friedrich Nietzsche,
Beyond Good and Evil

Everything with a manifest face
also possesses a hidden one.
Georges Bataille,
Alleluia: The Catechism of Dianus

Shattered, Denied, Reordered

Diagnosed with pulmonary tuberculosis in April 1942, Georges Bataille took a leave of absence from the job as a librarian that he had held at the Bibliothèque Nationale for close to twenty years. In late July he also left Paris to live in Boussy-Saint-Antoine in the home of the mother of his close friend Marcel Moré. There he finished writing his first acknowledged major work, *Inner Experience*, after which he moved on to Panilleuse, a small village in Normandy near Mantes and Tilly, for the duration of a cold, rainy fall before returning to Paris in mid-December. It is not too much to say that those solitary months in Panilleuse — when Bataille was sick, cold, wet, and profoundly alone with the spectre of death — served as a crucible for several key texts and textual strategies in his work. That fall he wrote portions of *The Little One*, *The Dead Man*, *The Oresteia*, *L'Archangélique*, *Guilty*, and an early draft of *The Accursed Share*, as well as

[81]

a number of poems, sketches and other writings. Though much of his thought and many of his textual strategies date back to the late 1920s and to shorter texts written in the 1920s and 30s — several of which were subsumed within *Inner Experience* prior to his arrival in Panilleuse — this period nevertheless marks a decisive breakthrough in Bataille's practice as a writer, particularly as a writer of poetry and fiction.

Returning to Paris in December 1942, Bataille remained there through March 1943 when he, Denise Rollin, and her young son, Jean, moved to the hilltop village Vézeley, where he would meet his future wife, Diana Kotchoubey de Beauharnois in June. That same month *The Little One* was published in an edition of 50 copies, though circulated only privately, by someone named Louis Trente.

The other texts begun in Panilleuse gestated in manuscripts, notes and drafts, often appearing partially at first, in journals and reviews, in luxurious editions with small printings, though also later in larger textual assemblages, alongside other writings. Several poems from *The Oresteia*, for example, appeared in an anthology, *Domaine français*, through Éditions des Trois Collines in 1943, others in *L'Éternelle Revue* in 1945 and in *Quatre Vents* that same year, before the collection was published in its entirety first by Éditions des Quartre Vents and later, with *The Story of Rats* and *Dianus*, as *La Haine de la Poésie* (The Hatred of Poetry) by Éditions de Minuit in 1947. The collection is now recognised as *The Impossible*, the title Bataille gave it for its second edition in 1962.

During this same period in the mid-1940s, Bataille finished *Guilty* — begun in notebooks in 1939, continued in Panilleuse, completed as a book in summer 1943 — and published it in early 1944, at which point he was already writing what would become *On Nietzsche* — completed in August 1944, published in February 1945. Like *Inner Experience* before them, these books present profoundly heterogeneous, hybrid constructions, including elements of diary and autobiography, poetry, a letter, a lecture, long quotations from other authors, as well as more recognizably philosophical and theological fragments. Measuring these books alongside the other works Bataille produced during this period extends and even radicalises this observation. While it is true that Bataille had already written several of his most famous narratives — *Story of the Eye, Blue of Noon, Madame Edwarda* — following the fall of 1942 and for the next three or more years, he turned to poetry and fictional prose with a new intensity and in some ways a new approach, producing his first full book of poems, *L'Archangélique*, the poetry and prose of *The Oresteia*, prose narratives including *The Dead Man, Julie, The Story of Rats*, and *Dianus*, as well as a portion of a play, *Le Prince Pierre*,[1] and even a draft screenplay, *La Maison Brulée*[2] (The Burned House).

Against this expansive, experimental literary horizon, it is not particularly surprising to learn that Bataille was also interested in having his work set to music. In

---

[1] Georges Bataille, *Oeuvres complètes*, ed. Thadée Klossowski (Paris : Gallimard, 1971) IV: 319-25.

[2] Bataille, *Romans et Récits*, ed. Jean-François Louette, et al. (Paris : Gallimard, Bibliothèque de la Pléiade, 2004) 945-75.

October and November 1944, he was sharing an apartment in Paris with composer René Leibowitz. Leibowitz later told Thadée Klossowski, an editor of Bataille's *Oeuvres Complètes*, that, "Bataille wrote these poems in front of me with the idea that I could perhaps set them to music." The manuscript held by Leibowitz includes the following:

> Songs:
> 1. The dregs [cf. *The Tomb of Louis XXX*]
> 2. My crack [cf. *The Little One*]
> 3. I have shit [cf. *The Little One*]
> 4. The wound [cf. *The Tomb of Louis XXX*
> 5. Night is my nudity [cf. *The Oresteia*]
>
> The Book [cf. *The Tomb of Louis XXX*]
> The Oratorio [cf. *The Tomb of Louis XXX*].

For our purposes it is significant to note that the poems Bataille gave Leibowitz come from three separate texts: *The Little One, The Tomb of Louis XXX*, and *The Oresteia*. Yet while Bataille may indeed have *copied* these poems for Leibowitz in the fall of 1944, he had already published at least portions of two of them the previous year in *The Little One*. Leibowitz's account nevertheless signals the proximity — indeed the commingling — of these texts in Bataille's writing and thought at the time.

Before being too surprised that Bataille might have sought to have some of his work set to music, we should remember the significant if nevertheless minor place of music in his oeuvre. In 1936, the figure of Acéphale had been conceived by Bataille and André Masson essentially while listening to Mozart's *Don Giovanni*. He wrote: "At this very moment, I am watching this acéphalic being, this intruder composed of two equally excited obsessions, become the 'Tomb of Don Giovanni.'"[3] Extending this thought, in *Inner Experience*, he writes: "Don Juan is in my eyes… only a personal incarnation of the festival, the carefree orgy, which negates and divinely overturns obstacles."[4] Elsewhere in *Inner Experience*, he writes in praise of Beethoven's *Leonora* and of the transformative power of liturgical music.[5] Before becoming too high-minded, we should also remember that, as is testified in the texts collected here, Bataille was a devotee of the burlesque Concert Mayol.

Poetry and prose, film and music, autobiographical fact and speculative philosophy, theology and fiction: Financial need provides one at least partial explanation for this proliferation of genres and forms in Bataille's work during this period. On extended medical leave from the Bibliothèque Nationale, he needed the money. It is an ironic fact of the writer's life that writers with jobs often don't have the time or financial motive to write. Writers without jobs, however, starving artists, write out of necessity, to put bread on the table. The proliferation of genres and forms extends this logic as the writer looks for something, *anything* that will sell, ideally to as many audiences as possible. This in mind, it is not surprising that Bataille would experiment with more extended and arguably accessible, therefore

[3] Bataille, "The Sacred Conspiracy" (1936) in Bataille, *Visions of Excess: Selected Writings, 1927-1939* (Minneapolis: University of Minnesota Press, 1985) 181.

[4] Bataille, *Inner Experience* (1943) trans. Leslie Anne Boldt (Albany: SUNY Press, 1988) 77.

[5] See *Inner Experience*, 69 and 75-6.

profitable, narrative forms. He speaks in these terms in a letter to Michel Gallimard from September 1945, claiming that he has almost finished a novel, *Costume d'un Curé Mort* (The Clothes of a Dead Priest), that promises to be commercially profitable.[6] Such claims — even when considered in relative terms — may make us smile. As profoundly influential as they have been, Bataille's writings are hardly the stuff of which bestsellers are made, even in a more literate cultural context than our own. That in mind, while financial need may provide some measure of an explanation for the proliferation of genres, forms and strategies of publication in Bataille's work, it cannot fully justify or explain the phenomenon. And indeed it would be untrue to Bataille's philosophical position — or to the life he lived beyond utility — to believe that it could.

Moreover, as is plainly evidenced in the texts collected here, the multiplication of forms is apparent both *between* Bataille's texts and *within* them. Thus while *L'Archangélique* is a book of poems and *The Story of Rats* a prose narrative, *The Little One* and *The Tomb of Louis XXX* include both poetry and prose, elements of fiction and elements of autobiography, as well as philosophical and theological meditations. These texts, like *Inner Experience*, *Guilty*, *On Nietzsche* and, more closely still, *The Oresteia*, are complex textual assemblages, hybrid texts that commingle forms and genres to produce their effects.

---

[6] See Bataille, *Choix de lettres*, ed. Michel Surya (Paris: Gallimard, 1997) 247. The novel in question may is related to both *La Scissiparité* (1949) and *L'Abbé C.* (1950).

From his earliest writings, Bataille used strategies of generic hybridity and textual assemblage. *Story of the Eye* includes both a "story" and a frame text, entitled "Coincidences" in the 1928 edition of the work and "Reminiscences" in later editions. *Blue of Noon* — written largely in 1935, but rewritten and published in 1957 — begins with a section from *W.C.* written prior to 1927, discussed in *The Little One*, and published separately as "Dirty" by Éditions Fontaine in 1945. But *Blue of Noon* also includes, in a crucial though brief first part, an article that is at least partially autobiographical, written in 1934, originally published in the journal *Minotaure* in 1936, and later included in *Inner Experience* in 1943. Similarly, the third part of *Inner Experience* consists almost entirely of previously published texts like this one strung together by autobiographical and other commentary. Bataille's work as an editor of *Documents* (1929-30), *Acéphale* (1936-39), and *Critique* (1946-1962), among other endeavours, undoubtedly also reflects his interest in textual assemblage as a productive creative enterprise.

In *Theory of Religion* — another text left unpublished during his lifetime, another text assembled *from* other texts (a lecture) and *with* other texts (other lectures and essays) as part of an abortive volume of *La Somme Athéologique* — Bataille writes on the subject of assemblage: "the work of the mason, who assembles, is the work that matters. Thus the adjoining bricks, in a book, should not be less visible than the new brick, which is the book. What is offered the reader, in fact, cannot be an element, but must be the ensemble in which it is inserted: it is the whole human assemblage and edifice, which must be, not just a pile of scraps, but rather a self-consciousness. In a sense the unlimited assemblage is the impossible."[7] A book, in other words, is never an autonomous unit, it always appears with and within a more or less visible, complex network of texts and contexts. Unlimited assemblage is the impossible because the whole human assemblage and edifice remains forever elusive to individual consciousness. According to Bataille, "Language scatters the totality of all that touches us most closely even while it arranges it in order. Through language we can never grasp what matters to us, for it eludes us in the form of interdependent propositions, and no central whole to which each of these can be referred ever appears. Our attention remains fixed on this whole but we can never see it in the full light of day."[8] Fleeting glimpses of an ever-changing, emergent ensemble describe the limits of our consciousness.

On this point it is poignant and to the point to remember that Walter Benjamin left his manuscripts in Bataille's care at the Bibliothèque Nationale — including the manuscripts for what was to be *The Arcades Project* — when he fled Paris for the Spanish frontier in the spring of 1940. Bataille would later unsuccessfully attempt to publish the materials on behalf of his friend. Related to this we might also recall Bataille's admiration for a lecture Sergei Eisenstein gave at the Sorbonne in January 1930 in which Eisenstein spoke of the dialectic

---

[7] Bataille, *Theory of Religion* (1948) trans. Robert Hurley (New York: Zone Books, 1989) 9.

[8] Bataille, *Eroticism* (1957) trans. Mary Dalwood (San Francisco: City Lights Books, 1986) 274.

of forms that he was attempting to elaborate in his cinema. Bataille wrote: "The expression of the philosophical dialectic through forms, such as the maker of the film *Battleship Potemkin* [...] intends to carry out in his next film [...] may take on the value of a revelation, and determine the most elementary and thus consequential human relations. Without broaching here the question of the metaphysical foundations of any given dialectic, one can affirm that the determination of a dialectical development of facts as *concrete* as visible forms would be literally overwhelming."[9] For Bataille, the dialectic of forms is a dialectic of material forms in nature but it is also a dialectic of visual and discursive forms elaborated against the background of similar developments by Benjamin, Eisenstein and others.

The Tomb of Louis XXX marks one apotheosis of assemblage in Bataille's corpus. It begins with poems, presents an impossibly brief "Oratorio," a section entitled "The Book" that consists of a poem and a photograph, and a "Meditation" that is aphoristic and autobiographical, speculative and reflective by turns, and that again includes a photograph. The brevity of the work bespeaks the intensification of its strategies, which stand in stark relief. The genres have been reduced to their elemental forms; the whole assembled as a prismatic constellation of competing, mutually reflective discourses and discursive gestures. What is

---

9 Bataille, "The Deviations of Nature" (1930) in *Visions of Excess*, 56. Eisenstein's lecture is available as "The Principles of the New Russian Cinema" (1930) in Eisenstein, *Selected Works: Volume 1: Writings, 1922-1934* ed. Richard Taylor (London: BFI, 1988) 195-202.

communicated is as much between the discourses as within them.

In Bataille's work and elsewhere, this play of genres and forms may be summarised and understood as the play of discourses and types of knowledge, wherein each type of writing brings with it a range of stylistic tropes and possibilities, as well as referential and epistemological assumptions and limitations. What can be said in one form might be horrifying or even explicitly forbidden in another. The novelist or poet may often venture where the theologian or philosopher should fear to tread.

Bataille was acutely sensitive to these concerns even as he exploited and accelerated their effects in and through his writing and indeed his career. The distinction between writing and career here is significant or at least mutually informative. As a writer, Bataille produced novels and poetry as well as essays, reviews, and extended works in fields ranging from anthropology and art history to philosophy, theology, political economy and religion. He also founded and edited several seminal journals of interdisciplinary inquiry: *Documents*, *Acéphale*, and *Critique*. To consider his career as a whole, however, multiplies this range of experience even further to include his work as an archivist and librarian, as a political militant and organiser, as well as his role as a founder and speaker in groups like Acéphale, the Society for Collective Psychology, the College of Sociology, and the Socratic College. After World War Two, Bataille continued to participate in a wide range of public lecture forums like the Club Maintenant and the Collège Philosophique, addressing both specialised and general audiences. In each case, every forum has its format and therefore its form. The production of effects in each distinct discursive space requires attention to these formal matters. My point here is also to observe that Bataille's corpus includes his writing, his editorial work, *and* all of his other activities, rather than just his writing. For some writers, the life lived alongside the literature is of no consequence — trust the tale not the teller, D.H. Lawrence said — but, in Bataille's case, the emphasis is on the *effects* produced rather than the objects produced. His entire corpus is an assault on the concept of autonomy, whether of individuals, objects, images or texts.

Of his work and his purpose, Bataille wrote: "If one had to grant me a place in the history of thought, I believe it would be that of having discerned the effects, in our human life, of the 'disappearance of the discursive real,' and of having drawn a senseless light from the description of these effects: this light is blinding, perhaps, but it announces the opacity of the *night*; it announces the night alone."[10] To speak of the disappearance of the discursive real is to speak of the collapse of discursive referentiality: no discourse, genre, or type of speech can — or should any longer — be taken to provide a stable means of reference to a commonly held understanding of reality. Language must be recognised as a language game. Bataille's move is to shift our attention away from the games pieces — the

---

[10] Bataille, "Post-Scriptum 1953," in *The Unfinished System of Nonknowledge*, ed. Stuart Kendall (Minneapolis: University of Minnesota Press, 2001) 206.

words — and away from the rules of the game — grammar, or in other cases specific taboos and transgressions — onto the effects produced by the game upon its player.[11] What matters is neither the game itself nor how one plays the game but the effects of playing the game. However humbling this recognition should be to our own speech, it is less significant in itself than it is in the effects it produces in our consciousness and lived experience.

There are several significant implications to this approach to language and experience. If there is no truth, no one type of speech that may convincingly convey a singular truth, everything is permitted. At its furthest limits this freedom of speech devolves into the babble of Babel, the kind of inconsequential language Bataille found as a fault in Surrealist automatic writing.[12] Speech becomes empty expression without social reference or the articulation of a relationship within a community of speakers. Fully free speech is speech with nothing left to say and no one to whom to say it, no one listening.

At another more literal extreme, the babble of tongues reflects the catastrophic collapse of basic communication in a global technological society, the cacophonous chaos of speech in the global village. Speaking of language in Auschwitz, Primo Levi offers a profound image of this problem in a passage from *Se questo è un uomo* (If This Is A Man): "The confusion of

---

[11] According to Bataille, "Language does not exist independently of the play of taboo and transgression," see *Eroticism*, 276.
[12] See *Inner Experience*, 148.

languages is a fundamental component of the manner of living here: one is surrounded by a perpetual Babel, in which everyone shouts orders and threats in languages never heard before, and woe betide whoever fails to grasp the meaning. No one has time here, no one has patience, no one listens to you; we latest arrivals instinctively collect in the corners, against the walls afraid of being beaten."[13] In one case, language is so free, so devoid of utility as to be empty of all effective content. In the other, that effective content is masked behind a failure of transference or translatability wherein the failure of communication opens a space of terror. In *Inner Experience*, Bataille wondered: "What happens to us when, disintoxicated, we learn what we are? Lost among babblers in the night in which we can only hate the appearance of light that comes from babbling. The self-acknowledged suffering of the disintoxicated is the subject of this book."[14] The same thing could be said of almost all of his work.

Indeed, Bataille's writing lays these structures bare. He does this through patient explanation, by writing across disciplines, by writing in different forms, and by assembling writings in the complex mechanisms that are his most far-reaching texts. "To write," he writes in *The Little One*, "is to research chance." It is to set the elements and structures of language free in the play of chance. But in Bataille's writing, this freedom is always animated and held in tension by the necessities of

---

[13]   Primo Levi, *Survival in Auschwitz* trans. Stuart Woolf (New York: Touchstone, 1996) 38.

[14]   *Inner Experience*, xxxii.

disciplinary limitation and discursive form, even as his orientation and language violates that form. "Transgression," he observes in *Eroticism*, "suspends a taboo without suppressing it."[15] Freedom is immanent, which is to say materially and ideologically informed and embodied: it is experienced only as an effect within and against a determinate horizon.

These notions outline a theory of experience in both descriptive and prescriptive ways: they provide the foundations of an ethos. Bataille claims: "I cannot consider someone free if they do not have the desire to sever the bonds of language within themselves."[16] Those bonds can never be severed permanently. Language is intrinsic to the human form and condition.[17] Listening to Alexandre Kojève's lectures on Hegel's *Phenomenology*, Bataille learned that "man becomes conscious of himself at the moment when — for the 'first' time — he says 'I.' To understand man by understanding his 'origin' is, therefore, to understand the origin of the I revealed by speech."[18] To sever the bonds of language within is to cause a disruption in self-consciousness, to dislocate the 'I' revealed by speech. This disruption might last no more than a moment.

During the spring of 1942, Bataille ended a lecture inaugurating a proposed "Socratic College" by

---

[15] *Eroticism*, 36.

[16] Bataille, "On the Subject of Slumbers," *The Absence of Myth*, 49.

[17] On language and human evolution, see Chris Stringer, *Lone Survivors: How We Came To Be The Only Humans On Earth* (New York: Times Books, 2012).

[18] Alexandre Kojève, *Introduction to the Reading of Hegel*, trans. James Nichols (New York: Basic Books, 1969) 3.

acknowledging, first, that any propositions about what he then called negative inner experience, could be shattered, denied, reordered; and, that second, any propositions that would follow could be shattered, denied, and reordered in their turn.[19] The ecstatic experience designated by the phrase "negative inner experience" in the lecture would become "inner experience" in the book of that title. By the time he wrote *On Nietzsche*, three years later, Bataille would say: "I don't want to continue speaking of *inner* (or mystical) experience right now but of *impalement*."[20] In *Method of Meditation*, written the following year, he would again change his terms: "Previously, I designated the sovereign operation under the names *inner experience* and *the extremity of the possible*. Now I designate it under the name of *meditation*. Changing the word signifies the anguish of using whatever word one might use."[21]

On this subject, in *The Unavowable Community*, Maurice Blanchot explains: "One must however not lose sight of the fact that one cannot be true to such a thought if one does not take into account Bataille's own infidelity, the necessary mutation which forced him to be unceasingly an other while remaining himself to develop other exigencies which resisted becoming united either because they responded to the changes of history or to experiences, which, not wanting to repeat themselves,

---

[19] "Socractic College," *Unfinished System of Non-Knowledge*, 17.
[20] *On Nietzsche*, 63; OC VI: 78.
[21] "Method of Meditation," *The Unfinished System of Nonknowledge*, 94. Bataille develops this theme most explicitly in his novel *L'Abbé C.* (Paris: Minuit, 1950).

had become exhausted."[22] This is finally a question of betrayal, betrayal of self, betrayal of designation, of nomination. Significantly, this wilful re-designation attests to the arbitrariness of the sign without analyzing the structure of that sign. Bataille's terminological shifts adhere to both a philosophical search for effective terms and the experiential demand for contagious language, a language of effects that forces change, which changes its speaker through the provocation of inner experience.

Method of Meditation

The articulation of a rigorous means of provoking inner experience, which is to say a method of meditation, was central to Bataille's concerns from the early 1920s on.[23] Particularly in the plans and writings associated with the secret society Acéphale and in the writings he associated with his unfinished project for *La Somme Athéologique*, from the abortive "Manual of an Anti-Christian" (1939)[24] through *Method of Meditation* (1947), Bataille demonstrated that intense, *sovereign* experiences, whether erotic, comic, aesthetic or ecstatic, could be provoked. Adapting techniques and elements of several traditions, Bataille situates his method within both

---

[22] Maurice Blanchot, *The Unavowable Community* (1983), trans. Pierre Joris (Barrytown, NY: Station Hill Press, 1988) 4.

[23] For a description of Bataille's early method of provoking waking dreams, see his letters to his cousin Marie-Louise Bataille, sent from Spain in spring 1922. Bataille, *Choix de lettres, 1917-1962* ed. Michel Surya (Paris: Gallimard, 1997) 26-28.

[24] See OC II: 377-402.

Eastern and Western traditions of mystical meditation: he borrows not only from Christianity but from Yoga and Zen as well. In *Guilty*, he wrote: "The traditional precepts are irrefutable; they are marvellous. I got them from one of my friends, who got them from an Oriental source. I am not unaware of Christian practices: they are more authentically dramatic."[25]

The designation "dramatic" is among the keys to understanding Bataille's meditative practice. It derives from the Christian meditative practices developed by the founder of the Jesuit order, Ignatius de Loyola. In *Inner Experience*, Bataille recounts Loyola's "dramatic" method in the following way: "The disciple of Saint Ignatius creates for himself a theatrical representation. He is in a peaceful room: [But] asked to have the feelings he would have on Calvary."[26] For Christians, the image of Christ on the cross epitomises both suffering and devotion. It is a scene and image that Bataille analyzes at length in *On Nietzsche*: "The killing of Jesus Christ is held by Christians as a group to be evil. It is the greatest sin ever committed. [...] Criminals are not the only actors in this drama, the fault falls to all humans. Insofar as someone does evil (every one of us being *required* to do evil), that person puts Christ on the cross."[27] Everyone, in other words, is implicated; everyone is guilty.

In Loyola's dramatic method of meditation, the believer becomes an actor, a stand-in for his or her God, a participant in the will to be everything. But taking the

---

[25] Bataille, *Guilty* (1944, 1961) trans. Stuart Kendall (Albany: SUNY Press, 2011) 32.

[26] *Inner Experience*, 119.

[27] *On Nietzsche*, 17, translation modified.

passion of the Christ on as one's own means accepting the death of God as the death of self. As Bataille says: "This sacrifice *which we consummate* is distinguished from others in this way: the one who sacrifices is himself affected by the blow which he strikes — he succumbs and loses himself with his victim."[28] Meditations, like those described by Loyola, propose the annihilation of the meditating subject alongside that of the subject of meditation. This reading effects a reversal of the Christian doctrine that Christ died for the sins of humanity. Traditionally, lacking the will to stand-in for one's God, to become everything, the Christian allows Christ to die for his or her sins. Faith in Christ's sacrifice absolves the believer of his or her sins, offering that believer the promise of salvation from suffering and death: Christ died (experienced death) so we do not have to. For Bataille, however, the Christian must *share* the fate of his or her deity, rather than allowing that deity to stand-in for his or her suffering: "In the end, one must see everything with lifeless eyes, one must become God, otherwise we would not know what it is to sink, to no longer know anything."[29]

One can begin to understand the place and function of self-consciousness and self-image in the meditative and even fictional writings of Georges Bataille in light of these reflections on drama and identification. For Bataille, as in the Christian model, the process of meditation entails the identification of the subject and the object (of meditation). The subject recognises

[28] *Inner Experience*, 153.
[29] *Inner Experience*, 153.

himself in the sacrificial object and thereby becomes what Bataille calls a "self-that-dies."[30] It is the megalomania of this subject to assume the position of God. Here the sacrificial lamb has a human face that is all too familiar. In *Inner Experience*, Bataille is emphatic on this point: "the object in experience is at first the projection of a dramatic loss of self. It is the image of the subject."[31] The subject then effects a division within himself through projection. Significantly however, this projection remains dramatic, rather than absolute. The projected self-image offers no new foundation for — or standard of — truth (as it does in the Christian model). Rather, the self dissolves in a catastrophe of infinite doubt, an abyss strung between identical extremes, neither of which can be true, though each of which functions — if only momentarily — as a necessary illusion in the game of truth that is the (dis)articulation of subjectivity. The "self-that-dies" is the self that dissolves in the ecstatic experience of this movement.

Bataille's method of meditation begins with the mental projection of his self-image. The goal of this projection is an impossible identification, identification with the impossible. Failing: this projection effects a division within the subject, a split within the real that reveals the real for what it is: an illusion. Rimbaud's modernist dilemma — "I is an other" — here becomes a mantra not a lament, or rather a lament as a mantra, a device of corrosive nostalgia. Doubt — the beating heart and will of the Cartesian subject — overwhelms the

---

30 *Inner Experience*, 71.
31 *Inner Experience*, 117.

stable limits of the subjective ego, vertigo ensues, and the ego falls away or implodes in a frenzy of failed identification. Bataille describes the moment: "The point, before me, reduced to the most paltry simplicity, is a person. At each instant of experience, this point can radiate arms, cry out, sets itself ablaze."[32] The subject fails to identify, in the Hegelian sense, with the totality of the world, fails to become everything, and in this failing, recognises the essential solitude of human subjectivity, a solitude that comes into being or can be recognised only just this side of the impossible, in the tragic failure of freedom. In meditation, the subject contests his or her limits, values, possibilities. Experience designates the moment when these limits open onto limitlessness, when possibilities open onto the impossible.

The violence of this moment is neither masochistic nor sadistic in the clinical sense. The pleasure of meditation is not the pleasure of an ego in relentless self-expansion or submission. The clinically sadistic ego achieves ecstasy through a successful identification with immanent pulsionary or material animality. Bataille's "self-that-dies" on the other hand uncovers the pleasures of a will pushed beyond its breaking point, the pleasures of the abyss.

Images are key: Bataille's dramatic method requires the projection of images in the imagination. Meditation begins with the projection of a self-image as a "self-that-dies" and ends with the dissolution of that image. Toward this end, images of human transport, whether

---

[32] *Inner Experience*, 118.

through ecstasy or suffering, serve as signposts on the road to catastrophe. As vehicles of meditation, images of laceration serve to effect the laceration of images. Bataille writes: "I'm going to say how I attained so intense an ecstasy. On the wall of appearances, I projected images of explosion, of laceration. First I had to create the greatest silence within myself."[33] Bataille's fascination with extreme states is the opposite of fetishism, or, perhaps more aptly put, it tears its fetishes to shreds.

In his final work, *The Tears of Eros* (1961), Bataille provides additional contextual information: "In 1938, a friend initiated me into the practice of yoga. It was on this occasion that I discerned, in the violence of [an image of Chinese torture victim, Fou Tchou Li], an infinite capacity for reversal. Through this violence [...] I was so stunned that I reached the point of ecstasy. My purpose is to illustrate a fundamental connection between religious ecstasy and eroticism — and in particular sadism. From the most unspeakable to the most elevated [...] the contraries appear to be linked."[34] As in William Blake, the marriage of heaven and hell celebrates the union of opposites, the proximity of horror and delight. On this point, writing about André Gide, Bataille notes: "We should, as Gide wanted to, marry within ourselves Heaven and Hell: this requires that the purity of Heaven be maintained."[35] But

---

[33] *Guilty*, 28.
[34] Bataille, *The Tears of Eros*, trans. Peter Connor (San Francisco: City Lights Books, 1998) 206-7.
[35] OC XII: 139.

differently in *The Little One*, "Innocence is the love of sin."

In *The Tomb of Louis XXX*, Bataille again references the photograph of the Leng Tch'e: "In that unexpected state, the memory of this photograph came to my mind without provoking the habitual depression: a rush of horror, of light, brought me from the depths to the heights. Nothing exceeds the feeling inspired in me by torture more."

The ecstasy of inner experience need not only follow from meditations on violent themes. In *Method of Meditation*, Bataille describes an ensemble of what he calls sovereign behaviours including but not limited to: "[religious] ecstasy, drunkenness, eroticism, laughter, sacrificial effusion, poetic [or aesthetic] effusion."[36] In each case, the process and results are unique, though the experience provoked remains similarly fleeting, useless, and thoughtless: "In laughter, sacrifice or poetry, even partly in eroticism, effusion is obtained through a modification, willing or not, in the order of objects: poetry makes use of changes on the level of images; sacrifice, in general, destroys things; laughter results from diverse changes. In drunkenness, on the contrary, the subject himself is willingly modified: it is the same in meditation."[37] The key to each behaviour is the rupture it affects within the realm of thought, of spiritual transcendence. Where experience alone is the sole value and authority, no single method or means of attaining

36 *Method of Meditation*, 218.
37 *Method of Meditation*, 219.

experience may hold priority.[38] Experience alone matters. And the structure of inner experience does not change: experience, whether provoked by laughter, eroticism, meditation or drunkenness always involves the dissolution of the subject, the transformation of the subject into a "self-that-dies."

In the third part of *Inner Experience*, "Antecedents to the Torture (or the Comedy)," Bataille relates an incident that took place during the summer of 1934. While travelling through Italy in an attempt to regain his health after a rheumatic crisis, Bataille found himself staying in Stresa, on the Lago Maggiore. Exhausted from ill health and travel, he sits on a bench on the pontoon bridge across the lake, and is struck by the majestic beauty of the mountains, the sunlight reflected off the water. The moment intensifies when he hears celestial voices: he quickly realises that a choir is singing mass in a near-by church, and that loudspeakers are broadcasting the music across the lake. Despite this knowledge, he is transported by the incongruous yet complementary beauty of the setting and the music, the natural beauty of the mountains and lake, of the sun, the sky, and the "human" beauty of that most refined of hymns, a hymn in praise of God which, through its complexity, betrays the independence and will of its human creators. The music embodies the history and tradition of the Catholic church, and, despite this affiliation, the atheologian is moved by its "superhuman power": "The sacred nature of the incantation only strengthened a sense of power, proclaimed to the sky

---

[38] *Inner Experience*, 7.

despite itself, to the point of laceration, the presence of a being exultant in its certitude and as though assured of infinite chance. (It mattered little that this was born of the ambiguity of Christian humanism; nothing mattered anymore — the choir cried out with superhuman power."[39] The contrast here between the immanent material continuum of the natural world and the complexity of the human creation — the tradition it embodied, the beauty of its form, etc. — provoked the revelry of inner experience, if not exactly the ecstatic frenzy normally associated with such experiences. It might also be noted that this experience relied upon the power of technology — specifically the technological mediation of the loudspeakers broadcasting the mass — to bring about its effect. This technological aspect goes unremarked by Bataille but it may be incorporated in our appreciation of that complex human creation.

Meditation requires contestation, and contestation — thought revelling in tragic complementarity — requires and results from textual and experiential heterogeneity. Bataille's sensitivity to and exploration of generic, disciplinary and institutional distinctions and his attention to various bodily practices (eroticism, yoga) all testify to this problematic. In this light, the radical interdisciplinarity of Bataille's work can be understood as an attempt to grasp the totality of experience in an age of increasing specialization *and* as a means to provoke meditative experience through contestation. These strategies of experiential and literary contestation are most clearly evident in his most radically heterogeneous

---

[39] *Inner Experience* 76 tm; OC V: 91.

writings, like *The Little One* and *The Tomb of Louis XXX*. The contestation embodied in these texts begins with the author's name.

The Names of Georges Bataille

There are perhaps as many reasons for pseudonymous publication in modern literature as there are examples of it. Some of the most famous are also closest to Bataille and to the works under consideration here. Isidore Ducasse, for example, published his own cantos of evil under the pseudonym the Comte de Lautréamont and Bataille was reading *The Concept of Anxiety* by *Vigilius Haufniensis*, a.k.a. Søren Kierkegaard, during the period when he was writing *The Little One* in particular. While Bataille's frequent use of pseudonyms is well known, it is rarely taken as seriously as, for example, Fernando Pessoa's elaborate system of heteronyms. The presentation of *Madame Edwarda* and *The Little One* in Bataille's *Oeuvres Complètes*, for example, makes no overt reference to the pseudonymous publication of these texts: the details are buried in the fine print of notes at the back of the book. Similarly, the Pléiade edition of Bataille's collected novels and tales, *Romans et Récits*, omits *The Tomb of Louis XXX* altogether, most likely for formal reasons, though it is included in the volume of his *Oeuvres Complètes* devoted to posthumous literary works. These obfuscating omissions are undoubtedly small oversights, but they are symptomatic of the reductive, hegemonic ideologies of discursive form and authorship under consideration here.

Bataille clearly ruminated upon his pseudonyms, explained them, and, as in the case of Louis Trente, developed them as identities across multiple, discontinuous and distinct works. Most often, I think, Bataille's use of pseudonyms is understood too quickly as a feint deployed to evade prosecution for violating censorious laws. Indeed, in the case of *Story of the Eye*, Bataille's recourse to the pseudonym Lord Auch can be partially explained by the strict censorship laws then in place in France and by his status as a librarian at the Bibliothèque Nationale and hence also as a civil servant. Had he been prosecuted for publishing pornographic literature he would have lost his job. This same argument holds for the publication of "L'Amitié" (Friendship) under the pseudonym Dianus in *Mesures* in 1940, of *Madame Edwarda* under the pseudonym Pierre Angélique in December of 1941, and of *The Little One* under that of Louis Trente in June 1943. Censorship laws slackened somewhat in the immediate aftermath of World War Two, but Bataille still had trouble publishing some of his erotic works with large houses, like Gallimard, whose printers refused to print certain works on "moral" grounds.[40] As with the argument that financial need motivated Bataille's formal experimentation, the argument that censorship — and the financial threat behind it — motivated his recourse to pseudonyms explains his use of them too easily. Arguments like these explain the gesture from the

[40] See note four to Bataille's November 1st, 1945 letter to Michel Gallimard, in Bataille, *Choix de lettres: 1917-1962*, ed. Michel Surya (Paris: Gallimard, 1997) 253.

outside, as a limitation, rather than from the inside, demonstrating the creative use Bataille made of that limitation.

Bataille's strategies of pseudonymous publication as well as the different types of information carried by the pseudonyms themselves help us understand this gesture and its effects in the case of Louis Trente. In *The Little One*, Louis Trente attributes *W.C.* — the book he wrote a year before *Story of the Eye* — to someone named Troppmann. The name will reappear as that of the protagonist of *Blue of Noon*. It derives from Jean-Baptiste Troppmann, who murdered a family of eight and was executed for his crimes in 1870, but it suggests, in a French language pun, *trop* or "too much" man. Rimbaud and Lautréamont both mention Troppmann their works.

The pseudonym Lord Auch from *Story of the Eye* is described alongside Troppmann in *The Little One* and is thus subsumed by the authorial purview of Louis Trente, who informs us that the name "recalls the habit of a friend of [Louis Trente's]: when irritated, he said, 'aux chiottes!' [*to the shithouse*], or even shortened this to say 'aux ch." Lord in English means God (in holy writings): Lord Auch is God relieving himself." The moniker is as blasphemous as the *Story* to which it is attached and as blasphemous as Louis Trente, who writes: "This God who animates us under swarming clouds is mad. I know it, I am this God."

During the same period in which Bataille was writing *Story of the Eye* (published in 1928), he was also writing and rewriting drafts of a visionary text elaborating the myth of a "pineal eye." "The eye," he wrote in one draft, "at the summit of the skull, opening on the incandescent sun in order to contemplate it in a sinister solitude, is not a product of the understanding, but is instead an immediate existence: it opens and blinds itself like a conflagration, or like a fever that eats the being, or more exactly the head… this myth is identified not only with life but with the loss of life — with degradation and death."[41] These drafts culminated in the publication of "The Solar Anus" in 1931, the crucial figure of which is the Jésuve, a name commingling *je* (or I in French), Jesus, and Vesuvius. "I am the Jésuve," Bataille writes, "the filthy parody of the torrid and blinding sun."[42] "The Solar Anus" did not appear under a pseudonym but, as should be clear from the components of the name itself, the mythic figure of the Jésuve, like Acéphale later, stands in the genealogy of the Little One, Louis Trente.

A decade later, in 1940, when Bataille published selections from his notebooks under the title "L'Amitié" (Friendship) in Jean Paulhan's journal *Mesures*, he did so under the pseudonym Dianus. "It seemed impossible to publish them under my own name," he wrote almost twenty years later still in notes for a preface to the second edition of *Guilty*, where the selections were reprinted under his own name. "The name chosen was that of a great Latin god, Janus or Dianus, that then responded to the religious but paradoxical atmosphere in which I lived."[43] Janus, the two faced god; Dianus, a name carrying within itself the words *Dieu* (God) and

---

[41] Bataille, "The Pineal Eye" (1927-31), *Visions of Excess*, 82.
[42] Bataille, "The Solar Anus" (1927), *Visions of Excess*, 9.
[43] *Guilty*, 158.

anus. In notes for *Inner Experience* from summer 1942, Bataille wrote: "The pseudonym Dianus seems to me to reunite the flavour of a bearded woman and that of a dying god, throat streaming with blood."[44]

Dianus also invokes the Tauric Diana, the goddess whose celebrated priest at Nemi is better known as the King of the Wood. This is the haunted figure whose priesthood begins with the murder of the previous priest and ends with his own murder by the subsequent one. In one version of the myth Orestes instituted the priesthood when he fled to the lake at Nemi seeking absolution for a murder. Sir James George Frazer tells his story in *The Golden Bough*. Bataille visited the lake in April 1934. In *Guilty*, he adopts the persona of the priest in the final section, "The Divinity of Laughter," written in 1943: "I am the king of the wood, Zeus, the criminal... My desire? Unlimited... Could I be *Everything*? I can be — laughably... [...] In the depths of the wood, as in the bedroom where two lovers are undressing, laughter and poetry are liberated."[45] In *The Oresteia*, he adopts the persona of Orestes in flight, while the other two texts from *The Impossible* develop the fictional identity of Dianus in *The Story of Rats (The Journal of Dianus)* and *Dianus*.[46]

Finally, in regard to the name Dianus, one may speculate as to the role it played in Bataille's life in June of 1943, when he met and fell in love with his future wife: the fictional Dianus met the real Diana

---

[44] *Inner Experience*, 186.
[45] *Guilty*, 105.
[46] *The Impossible*, 83-117.

Kotchoubey de Beauharnois. *Alleluia: The Catechism of Dianus*, the text he appended to the second edition of *Guilty* for inclusion in *La Somme Athéologique*, was likely to have been written in letters responding to questions from her that fall or the following spring. It was published in 1947 in two versions — one with illustrations by Jean Fautrier, one without illustrations.[47]

Dianus is thus a name that crosses curious frontiers in Bataille's writing, used first perhaps to avoid problems with censorship in 1940, the writings which bear the name were later published under Bataille's own signature. In 1944, the first edition of *Guilty* began with a note: "Someone named Dianus wrote these words and died. He designated himself (paradoxically) by the name the guilty one." The note was signed with the initials G.B.[48] Later the name Dianus would designate a fictional persona, in *The Story of Rats* and *Dianus*, as well as the author of *Alleluia: The Catechism of Dianus*. Fact and fiction are so closely entwined in the name that it may be impossible to separate them, particularly in *The Story of Rats*.

Pierre Angélique is in some ways more straightforward. He signed *Madame Edwarda*, a text written in September and October of 1941 and published in December of that year. The name may derive from that of the divine Angela of Foligno (c. 1248-1309), the saint whose *Book of Visions* "gripped [Bataille] to the point of trembling" when he read it in

[47] *Guilty*, 131-50.
[48] *Guilty*, 3.

September 1939.[49] Pierre also means stone in French, a notion perhaps reflected in *The Tomb of Louis XXX* when God speaks from a stone. *Madame Edwarda* was reprinted several times during Bataille's lifetime, most notably in 1956, when he signed a preface to a new edition with his own name. While preparing the preface, Bataille wrote additional texts expanding the fictional story of Pierre, *My Mother* and *Charlotte d'Ingerville* (both 1955). These would be his last fictions.

As with Bataille's other pseudonyms, the name Louis Trente is over-determined. The name Louis almost certainly derives from that of French kings, most notably Louis XVI who was guillotined at the peak of the French Revolution on January 21st, 1793. Louis here stands in for the last true sovereign of France and he should be recognised alongside the mythic Acéphale as a headless man. Bataille's fascination with Louis circles around the site of his beheading, the Place de la Concorde in Paris where the obelisk of Luxor is now located. In 1938, he wrote: "From Louis XVI's guillotine to the obelisk, a spatial arrangement is formed on the PUBLIC SQUARE, in other words, on all the public squares of the 'civilised world' whose historical charm and monumental appearance prevail over everything else. For it is nowhere but THERE that a man, in some ways bewitched, in some ways overtaken by frenzy, expressly presents himself as 'Nietzsche's madman' and illuminates with his dream-lantern the mystery of the DEATH OF GOD."[50] In the notebooks that would

---

[49] *Guilty*, 14.
[50] Bataille, "The Obelisk" (1938), *Visions of Excess*, 213.

become *Guilty*, Bataille recounts an episode from 1936, when he and three friends planned to spill a flask of blood at the base of the obelisk alongside a note signed under the pseudonym of the Marquis de Sade directing its readers to the location of a skull — softened through chemical treatment — alleged to be that of Louis XVI. Nothing came of the plan. "I only offer it," he wrote, as I do, "as testimony to a durable obsession."[51]

Louis' surname is equally freighted with meaning. In French, Trente means 30, hence the equation between the Louis Trente who wrote *The Little One* and the Louis XXX buried in *The Tomb of Louis XXX*. Louis Trente or Louis XXX can thus also be understood as Louis the 30th, a fictitious continuation of the line of the Bourbon kings.

But Trente is also French for Trento, the city in northern Italy. Historically, Trento is best known as the site of the *Concilium Tridentinum*, the Catholic Council of Trento, convened by Popes Paul III, Julius III, and Pius IV in three successive periods between December 13, 1545 and December 4, 1563. During the 25 sessions of the Council, its members issued seventeen dogmatic decrees addressing all aspects of Catholicism — defining for its time concepts such as sin, salvation, and the Eucharist — and answering the challenges proposed by the Protestant Reformation. The Council of Trento was the major doctrinal push of the Catholic Counter-Reformation and its decrees stood at the centre of the faith for four hundred years, until Pope John XXIII convened Vatican II beginning in 1962. Louis Trente is

---

[51] *Guilty*, 172-3.

Louis Trento, burdened with the conceptual weight of the Catholic Council of Trento. The God of *The Little One* and *The Tomb of Louis XXX* should be understood in Catholic terms or as a heresy of them.

But Trento also has personal meaning for Georges Bataille. He spent the night of July 25th, 1934 there with Colette Peignot, who had become his lover and who would become his companion, at first off and on, then devotedly, until her death on November 7th, 1938. Colette, who is better known by her middle name, Laure, had been travelling in Italy and the Alps with her then lover and companion Boris Souvarine, from whom, on this night, she would begin to separate. Bataille was himself in the process of separating from his wife of six years, Sylvia. The night in Trento, in other words, was an impassioned night of commitments and betrayals, of endings and beginnings, and Bataille came to recognise it as crucial in his recognition of his own biological solitude. The moment was also overcast with dark clouds of looming political catastrophe. The year had begun with the suicide-alleged-murder of Alexandre Stavinsky and a general strike in France and — on the very night Bataille and Laure spent in Trento — the Chancellor of Austria, Engelbert Dollfuss, was assassinated by Nazi agents.[52]

Bataille recounted the night in a short text entitled "Blue of Noon," dated August 1934. He first published the text in the journal *Minotaure* in 1936 but it also served as Part One of Bataille's novel of the same name,

---

[52] For additional biographical information and context, see Stuart Kendall, *Georges Bataille*, 104-117.

written primarily in May 1935. Bataille included the same short text in *Inner Experience* as one of the "Antecedents to the Torture."[53] This text — published three different times in three very different discursive locations: in a journal, a novel, and a work of philosophical theology — clearly possesses talismanic value in Bataille's corpus. As a record of the night from which at least part of the name of Louis Trente derives it is a crucial reference for understanding *The Little One* and *The Tomb of Louis XXX* as well.

In its earliest version, in *Minotaure*, the text begins with an evocation of the pineal eye before turning to the events of the night in Trento. Here is the passage concerned with that night:

"The ground will give way beneath my feet.

"I will die in hideous conditions.

"I take pleasure today from being the object of disgust for the sole being to whom destiny links my life.

"I solicit everything bad that a laughing man can receive.

"The exhausted head in which 'I' am has become so timid, so greedy that death alone could satisfy it.

"Several days ago, I arrived — really, not in a dream — in a town evoking the setting of a tragedy. One evening, I only say it to laugh in a more unhappy way, I was not alone, drunk, watching two old man turning while dancing — really, not in a dream. During the night, the Commendatore came into my room; the afternoon (I was passing in front of his tomb) pride and irony incited me to invite him. The appearance of the ghost struck me with terror, I was a wreck; a second

---

[53] See *Blue of Noon*, 23-4 and *Inner Experience*, 77-80.

victim was recumbent beside me: a foam uglier than blood flowed from lips that disgust rendered similar to those of a dead woman. And now I am condemned to this solitude that I do not accept, that I don't have the heart to bear. Yet I have only a cry to repeat the invitation and, if I believe my anger, it would no longer be me, it would be the shadow of the old man who would go away.

"Beginning with an abject suffering, the insolence that slyly persists grows again, first slowly, then, in a flash, reaches the wave of a happiness affirmed against all reason.

"Prometheus moaned when a chaos of rocks fell on him.

"Don Juan was drunk with carefree insolence when he was swallowed by the earth.

"Today, beneath the dazzling light of the Sky, justice aside, this sickly existence, close to death, and yet real, abandons itself to the 'lack' that reveals its coming into the world.

"Completed 'being,' from rupture to rupture, after a growing nausea had delivered it to the void of the sky, has become no longer 'being' but wound, and even 'agony' of all that it is."[54]

Before passing on, we can also make note of a passage from *On Nietzsche* in which Bataille alludes to the night he and Colette Peignot spent in Trento. This passage was written at the end of May 1944, and it compares the night in Trento to a recent night spent in Vézeley with his future wife, Diane de Kotchoubey:

---

[54] *Inner Experience*, 79-80; *Blue of Noon*, 23-24; translation modified.

"A night of fascination similar to few nights that I have known.

"The horrible night at Trento (the old men, handsome, dancing like gods — the storm letting loose, while I watched, from a room in which hell… — the window opened on the dome and the palaces along the square).

"At night, the little public square at V, atop the hill, resembled *for me* the square at Trento.

"Nights in Vézeley, equally entrancing as the agonizing one.

"A decision confirmed by a poem about dice, written at Vézeley, is related to Trento.

"The particular night in the forest was no less decisive.

"Chance — an incredible series of chances — has been my companion for ten years now. Lacerating my life, ruining it, leading it to the edge of the abyss. Certain types of chance skirt the edge: with a little more anguish and chance would become its opposite"[55]

The manuscript of *On Nietzsche* makes it clear that the night in Trento referenced here is the night in Trento described above, in *Blue of Noon*.[56] In this passage, written in May 1944, Bataille remarks that chance has been his companion for ten years, a duration marked by the beginning of his relationship with Laure in 1934. The referenced poem about the dice is most likely this one, from *On Nietzsche*:

---

[55] Bataille, *On Nietzsche* (1945) trans. Bruce Boone (New York: Paragon House, 1992) 106-7; translation modified.
[56] OC VI: 408-9.

Oh the dice thrown
From the depths of a tomb
By the fingers of the slender night

Dice like birds of sunlight
Leap from drunken larks
I like an arrow
Escape from the night

Oh transparency of bones
My heart drunk with sunlight
Is the shaft of the night.[57]

How can we begin to understand this night in Trento? A night of fascination, a horrible night, agonizing; dreamlike, but real; a night set for a tragedy, but real. Tragedy: after the Greeks, after Racine, after Kierkegaard, after Nietzsche: the co-presence of irreconcilable opposites: Being torn between voids of earth and sky. A night of belonging and betrayal, of fidelity bound to infidelity. "The truth of eroticism," Bataille would later write, in another context, "is treason."[58]

The night in Trento was a night similar to few Bataille had known and that alone says something from a man famous among his friends for debauchery. It was a night through which he would come to recognise the right and power of chance over life. "Chance animates the smallest parts of the universe," he writes in *The Little One*. And, "knowing the secrets of words I maintain the

[57] *On Nietzsche*, 83 ; translation modified.
[58] *Eroticism*, 171.

bond of writing between chance and myself… To write is to research chance." Elsewhere in *The Little One*, the hegemony of chance is expressed in terms of the problem of time and of history: "If I give up my anxiety about a time to come, an intoxication with life follows remorse, drunkenness in one form or another. In the same way my concern for the future, if it's real, if it's anxious, differs in no way from remorse: one isn't afraid of suffering but of being guilty." In *Guilty*, Bataille quoted Nietzsche's *Gay Science* § 287 approvingly: "I love not knowing the future."[59] A few years later, in his essay "Initial Postulate," Bataille turns not knowing the future into a fundamental principle and the origin of a "discipline" which "would be to philosophy what a whole man is to a philosopher — or even, if you will, if he were a theologian, to God himself!"[60]

The night in Trento is also a night in which Bataille came to recognise, in a profoundly personal way, his essential solitude. In "Blue of Noon" as we saw above, he writes, "I am condemned to this solitude that I do not accept, that I don't have the heart to bear." Elsewhere he would frame this solitude in terms of the absence of community or belonging to the "community of those who have no community."[61] *The Little One* begins with a "festival for myself alone, at which, no longer able to maintain it, I break the tie that binds me to others." Just as Bataille argues that freedom of thought is predicated upon the ability to sever the bonds of language within

---

59 *Guilty*, 22.
60 Bataille, "Initial Postulate" (1947), in *The Unfinished System of Nonknowledge*, 108.
61 OC V: 483.

consciousness, he sees human freedom as fundamentally bound to the ability to sever the ties that bind us to others. "No one," he writes in *The Little One*, "loves who is not lead to break [this bond]." But this too is a principle of meditation, a starting place for thought and experience: "Perfect *derangement* (abandon to the absence of limits) is the rule of the *absence* of community."[62]

It is dangerous to push our reading of this night — and of the name that bears its mark in Bataille's oeuvre — too far. The night clearly possessed talismanic power for Bataille. The text "Blue of Noon" and the publication and republication of that text in *Minotaure*, *Inner Experience*, and *Blue of Noon* testifies to this power as does the name Louis Trente carried in different ways by *The Little One* and *The Tomb of Louis XXX*. But for Bataille, once again, the meaning of a name is less interesting than the task it performs.[63] Louis Trente is not Georges Bataille. He is a means by which Bataille may experience his own difference from himself. Ultimately Bataille's pseudonyms serve as masks in the drama of meditation, masks that produce effects as they are put on and taken off, as they displace apparently stable identities and demonstrate that I is an other.[64]

---

[62] Bataille, "Take It or Leave It" (1946) *The Absence of Myth*, ed. Michael Richardson (London: Verso, 1994) 96.

[63] See Bataille, "Formless," *Visions of Excess*, 31.

[64] It is perhaps significant to note that Bataille did not always use pseudonyms in so pointedly affective a way. During the late 1940s, he published a number of articles in *Critique* (founded in 1946) under pseudonyms. These pseudonyms include Saint-Melon-Léon, Noël Léon, Noël Laurent, Élie Chancelé, Édouard Menet, Henri-François Tecoz, and possibly others. Recourse to pseudonymity in this case can

Larvatus Prodeo

Larvatus Prodeo: a phrase from René Descartes' juvenilia. Come forward masked. "So far I have been a spectator in this theatre which is the world, but I am now about to mount the stage, and I come forward masked."[65] Descartes spoke from behind a mask in a time of religious persecution. It was part of his mask to carve the sciences into distinct disciplines, to separate spheres of knowledge, to speak boldly of metaphysics while advancing his analysis of the mechanics of physical force. Three hundred years later, in the time of the death of god, Bataille donned his mask for a different purpose, not to hide but to reveal.

Pseudonyms are masks that activate and are active within complex networks of meaning and association, personal, political, and linguistic. They accrete meaning as talismans but remain unstable, emergent and in play. A pseudonym is inserted into language as an act of intentional distantiation, an act that reveals and revels in the alienation of the autonomous self. A mask, according to Bataille, is "chaos become flesh. It is present before me like a fellow human being and this fellow being,

be explained more or less simply. It is often difficult for a new journal to find writers willing to appear its pages. Writing under pseudonyms helped Bataille to fill the journal in its first years without seeming to be the author of the majority of its content. For what may be only a selection of these articles, see Georges Bataille, *Une Liberté Souveraine*, ed. Michel Surya (Farrago, 2000).

[65] René Descartes, *The Philosophical Writings of René Descartes*, vol. 1, trans. John Cottingham, *et al.* (Cambridge: Cambridge University Press, 1985) 2.

which disfigures me, has taken on the figure of my own death; through this presence, chaos is no longer nature foreign to man but man himself animated by his pain and his joy which destroys man, man thrown into the possession of this chaos which is his annihilation and rot, man possessed by a demon, incarnating nature's intention to cause his death and rot. What is ceaselessly communicated from face to face is as precious and reassuring to human life as the light. When this communication is broken by the fact of a brutal decision when the face is returned by the mask to the night, man is no longer anything other than nature hostile to man and nature hostile to man is entirely animated by the underhanded passion of the masked man."[66] Hiding, as behind a mask, reveals that something is hidden. There is more here than meets the eye. In Bataille's terminology, from *Alleluia: The Catechism of Dianus,* "everything with a manifest face also possesses a hidden one."[67] But what is hidden is no more real than the mask. Quite the opposite in fact, the mask reveals the *absence* of that which is behind it.

In another sense, the mask is a mirror of the self, deployed to demonstrate the absence of the self. In *The Oresteia,* Bataille writes in the guise of Orestes: "It seemed to me yesterday that I spoke to my mirror."[68] The brothel in *Madame Edwarda* is called The Mirrors and in *Guilty* he admits: "A brothel is my true church."[69] The admission would be at home in *The Little One,*

66 Bataille, "Le masque," OC II: 404.
67 *Guilty,* 133.
68 *The Impossible,* 140.
69 *Guilty,* 10.

which takes its title from the language of the brothel designating what Bataille elsewhere calls the solar anus. The church and the brothel, for Bataille, mirror opposites and therefore contraries conjoined, from the most unspeakable to the most elevated, as in ecstasy and horror, in a hall of mirrors.[70]

The hall of mirrors is a hall of masks, a theater. In *The Oresteia*, Bataille writes, again in the guise of Orestes: "I open in myself a theater."[71] Later in the same text he quotes Kierkegaard, "My head is as empty as a theater in which there has just been a performance."[72] His poetics, like his method of meditation, is dramatic: the drama is a play of illusions, charades, a procession of masks or simulacra, in Pierre Klossowski's sense of this term.[73] Every word is a mask for the absence of clear and distinct meaning, for the free play of reference behind that word. Even the word God — in some senses the final word — is a mask indicating the absence of god. In *The Little One*, Louis Trente is emphatic: "In place of God... there is only the impossible, and not God."

---

[70] See *The Tears of Eros*, 206-7.

[71] *The Impossible*, 134.

[72] *The Impossible*, 143. For the quotation in context of Kierkegaard's works see, *Søren Kierkegaard's Journals and Papers, Part 1: Autobiographical, 1829-1848*, ed. and trans. Howard V. Hong and Edna H Hong (Indianapolis: Indiana University Press, 1978) 204. The quote in Kierkegaard differs slightly. It reads: "My head is as empty *and dead* as a theater in which there has just been a performance" [emphasis mine].

[73] See Pierre Klossowski, "Of the Simulacrum in Georges Bataille's Communication" in Leslie Anne Boldt Irons, ed. *On Bataille* (SUNY Press, 1995) 147-55.

The dramatic play of language as mask and revelation is literature. For Bataille, poetry — and indeed all literary writing — is a "sacrifice in which words are victims."[74] In literature, words are severed from their servile uses. Their stable meanings, supporting discourses, expected senses and referents fall away as potentialities, possibilities rather than certainties. Words are set free. This disruption of stable meanings and structured relationships is the opposite of good, clear and distinct, straightforward and serious writing; it is the evil that makes literature evil in the essays Bataille collected in *Literature and Evil*.

To pick only one small illustration of this, in *The Little One*, Bataille writes, parenthetically: "it's always night, it's always raining." The phrase stands out, opening a vein of imagination, contradicting all likely sense while conveying an impossible mood, the mood of the impossible. There is no situation that matches this description. The words anticipate the conclusion of Beckett's *Molloy*: "It was not midnight. It was no raining." Beckett's narrator fatally undermines his own reliability (he previously told us, "It is midnight. The rain is beating on the windows.")[75] In both cases, in Beckett and in Bataille, fiction is fiction and it announces itself as such. In literature, words are a problem. The purpose of this kind of writing is not to mediate a readers' relationship to a truth that the text somehow

---

[74] *Inner Experience*, 135.
[75] Samuel Beckett, *Molloy* (1947) in *Three Novels* (Grove Press, 1958) 92; 176.

represents. This kind of writing does not reveal a truth; it demonstrates the absence of any one truth.

A useful contrast might be drawn here between erotic writing, in Bataille's sense of both eroticism and writing, and pornography, including the obscene. Pornography — and here I am speaking of contemporary pornography, the pornography set free by the absence of censorship — presents a perfect surface, at once transparent and opaque, transparent in that the desiring subject must project his or her desires through it toward a space of pure imagination unencumbered by reference to reality, yet opaque in this same moment and for this same reason, because the surface of pornography does not point to *something* beyond itself; it points to *nothing* beyond itself; it is what it is and only what it is; its transparency is not transcendence. Pornography aspires to complete obscenity, to the condition of saying everything, revealing everything though only as a vehicle of desire. Obscenity no longer operates, as it once did, in a transgressive, dialectical manoeuvre, always seeking to show more. Now, in our time, pornography is obscene, nothing is hidden; all, or seemingly all, is revealed, and continuously available to anyone who cares to look. As Jean Baudrillard observes, "Pornography does not mask anything. It is not an ideology, i.e. it does not hide some truth; it is a simulacrum, i.e. it is a truth effect that hides the truth's non-existence."[76] But the effect of this absence is not the erotic effect produced by the absence of truth in Bataille's work.

[76] Jean Baudrillard, *Seduction*, trans. Brian Singer (New York: St. Martin's Press, 1990) 35.

[124]

Literary eroticism, erotica, in Bataille's practice, recalls the Greek understanding of the god Eros, described by Hesiod as "the most beautiful of the immortal gods, who in every man and every god softens the sinews and overpowers the prudent purpose of the mind."[77] Eros is desire where desire is the desire to soften and collapse distinctions between entities, including words, to commingle, conjoin and confound elements in the flow of life. Singular, isolated, stable meanings and identities are sacrificed, revealing the absence of *singular* meaning. While pornography is a caricature of desire; a stable structure that goes through the motions: erotica is the activation of desire, its implementation, wherein words, genres, discourses, images and texts, get on top of one another and become sexual. In *The Tomb of Louis XXX*, Bataille presents a poem facing a photograph of a woman's genitals: "I drink in your laceration/ and I spread your naked legs/ I open them as a book/ wherein I read that which kills me." The words and the image are at once baldly literal and boldly metaphoric and symbolic. The singularity of the manifest meaning opens up and gives way to the multiplicity of hidden meanings and the absence of any one truth. In *Alleluia: The Catechism of Dianus*, Bataille evokes a similar figure, insisting upon the specificity, the particularity of the manifest element: "The irreplaceable particularity is a finger pointing to the abyss, marking the immensity... the particularity is that of a woman showing her lover her *obscoena*. It is the index designating

---

[77] Hesiod, *Theogony*, trans. Norman O. Brown (Bobbs-Merrill, 1953) 56; lines 120ff.

the laceration, the mark of the laceration... The laceration would be nothing if it were not the laceration of a being, and precisely of a person chosen for his or her plenitude."[78] At stake is a relationship to *this* being, this person, this discourse, this name.

Through eroticism, and through the laceration that is the erotic image and text, biologically solitary beings become open to the being of the world in its multiplicity. Consciousness collapses into pure immanence. The textual or discursive remains of this immanent experience take the form of a cacophony of displaced and shattered voices like those of *The Little One* and *The Tomb of Louis XXX*. Bataille describes his experience pointedly: "The subject in experience loses its way, it loses itself in the object, which is itself dissolved. [...] Nonetheless, the subject in experience remains: To the extent that it is not a child in the drama, a fly on one's nose, it is *consciousness of others* [...] But it is no longer exactly the subject [...] By making itself *consciousness of others* and, as the ancient chorus, the witness, the populariser of the drama, it loses itself in human communication, as subject it is thrown outside of itself, beyond itself; it ruins itself in an undefined throng of possible existences."[79] The cold facts of discourse are replaced by the experience of communication. The ties that bind are broken and thereby stand revealed. Society is replaced with an experience of the community of those who have no community.

[78] *Guilty*, 145.
[79] *Inner Experience*, 61.

What became of Louis Trente? Bataille did not reprint *The Little One* after its original, small clandestine 1943 edition. He did not publish *The Tomb of Louis XXX* at all. If he had published this second text, would he have signed the text with his own name or with that of its eponymous subject?

Louis Trente was the last of Bataille's pseudonyms. Not the last to be used — since he continued the story of Pierre Angélique in *My Mother*, another unpublished text — but the last to be invented. Louis Trente was Bataille's last *new* name, his last new dramatic persona. Was Louis Trente too personal a name to be used publicly? Was it too obscure to be effective? Was Bataille simply trying to present his texts in a more accessible fashion, commercially speaking, to build a name for himself as an author of books? Whatever the case, whether for literary, historical, or biographical reasons, after Louis Trente, alongside Bataille's growing body of philosophical, anthropological and critical writings, there would be only fiction.

*

Translation is a curious kind of literary performance in which the words are someone else's. And yet, for all that, they do not belong entirely to that other. Speech in translation is speaking with someone else's tongue, the language tensed between at least two voices, as well as between languages and the communities implied by them. As may be obvious from the above, this book too is an assemblage gathered against itself, which is to say an evocation of the impossible. It seems fitting to end this discourse with words from someone else: "What, do you imagine that I would take so much trouble and so much pleasure in writing, do you think that I would keep so persistently to my task, if I were not preparing — with a rather shaky hand — a labyrinth into which I can venture, in which I can move my discourse, opening up underground passages, forcing it to go far from itself, finding overhangs that reduce and deform its itinerary, in which I can lose myself and appear at last to eyes that I will never have to meet again. I am no doubt not the only one who writes in order to have no face. Do not ask who I am and do not ask me to remain the same: leave it to our bureaucrats and our police to see that our papers are in order. At least spare us their morality when we write."[80]

Stuart Kendall

---

[80] Michel Foucault, *The Archeology of Knowledge* trans. A.M. Sheridan Smith (New York: Pantheon Books, 1972) 17.

Notes on the Text

These notes include editorials materials derived from Georges Bataille, Oeuvres complètes, ed. Thadée Klossowski (Paris: Gallimard, 1971) t. III: 495-500; t. IV: 384-86; and Georges Bataille, Romans et Récits, ed. Jean-François Louette et alia (Paris: Gallimard, Bibliothèque de la Pléiade, 2004) 1161-67. Cécile Moscovitz edited the section of Romans et Récits referenced here. I have amended, collated and modified the Gallimard notes for consistency and for an Anglophone readership. Editorial notes whether by the Gallimard editors or my own appear in italics. My own editorial notes are marked [Trans.].

The Little One

Louis Trente [Georges Bataille], Le Petit (no publisher listed [Georges Hugnet], 1934 [1943]); reprinted by Jean-Jacques Pauvert, 1963; reprinted in Bataille, OC III (Gallimard, 1971) 33-69; reprinted in Bataille, Romans et récits (Gallimard, 2004) 349-67.

Bataille first published The Little One *under the pseudonym Louis Trente in an edition of 50 copies with the help of writer, editor, publisher Georges Hugnet in June 1943. It was not commercially released but rather distributed by friends.*

Among Bataille's papers there is only a partial manuscript of The Little One *(Manuscript, 22 pages), extracts from a notebook, mixing outlines and various notes (in particular on* expenditure*). Two notebooks from 1942-43 (Notebook) contain: poems (notebook for* L'Archangélique*) and, along with notes for* The Accursed Share, *a draft of the final section, "A little later."*

[i] *"If no one had had the strength, at least while writing, to absolutely deny the link that attached him to his fellow men, we would not have the work of Sade." Georges Bataille,* The Accursed Share, vol. 2: The History of Eroticism, *trans. Robert Hurley (New York: Zone Books, 1993) pg. 175.*

[ii] *Manuscript:*

All is consummated, a pure ray of agony remains.

The universe itself envisioned as anguish.

God, the universe, it does not matter, but the wound of my soul in the depths of me, the dirty slipping, sticking and sudden fall, is the contrary of the *possible*: being *certain* but *impossible* at the same time.

The misrecognised sovereignty of the little one, its divinity from impossible certainty.

[iii] *Manuscript:*

I call despicable those who would not laugh at my death, who do not at least love to cry over me.

[iv] *Manuscript:*

If I had spoken intelligibly, I would have touched the depth of sufferings — where one can imagine no desirable way out, where the possible always has an absurd mask. God like a beast, tracked by the pack of necessities, the absence of limits.

[v] *Manuscript:*

he who has done as I have (like Mary and Jesus) a "little one"

[vi] *Manuscript:*

Freshness in the humid obscurity of a corridor… The hand slipped in between is the hand of *evil*.

[vii] *"Cock" here translates* la queue. *This word could also be translated as tail, rear or, more colloquially, arse.* Trans.

[viii] *"Pithiatic" here translates* pithiatique. *In 1901, Joseph Babinski renamed what Charcot's called hysteria as pithiatism, from the Greek words* peithos *(persuasion) and* iatos *(curable).*

[ix] *Alfred Maury (1817-92) is the author of* Sommeil et les Rêves (Sleep and Dreams) *[Paris, 1861]. The reference here is to pages 133-34.*

^x *Christian Wolff (1679-1754) and Auguste Comte* (1798-1857) *here stand in for university affiliated, positivistic philosophy and natural science.*

^{xi} *Søren Kierkegaard (1813-55), Danish philosopher and theologian.*

^{xii} *The "Introduction" to Bataille's* Blue of Noon *consists of at least one section from W.C., a section published by Editions Fontaine in the collection "L'Age d'Or" under the title* Dirty *as an independent narrative in 1945. Bataille is thus being somewhat disingenuous when he suggests that the manuscript was burned. At most it was burned only in part.* Trans.

^{xiii} *This story is also recounted in Georges Bataille, "Surrealism from Day to Day," see Bataille,* The Absence of Myth *(Verso, 1994) 41-3.*

^{xiv} *Henri Troppmann is the name of the main character in* Blue of Noon. *His surname derives from that of Jean-Baptiste Troppmann, who murdered a family of eight and was executed in January 1870. Troppmann's exploits figure in the poetry of Rimbaud and Lautréamont. In French, Troppmann is a pun suggesting "too much" "man."* Trans.

^{xv} *See Georges Bataille, "Le Cadavre Maternel" OC II: 130 and Bataille,* Blue of Noon *(London: Marion Boyars, 1986) 38 and 76. For further information see Stuart Kendall,* Georges Bataille (Reaktion Books, 2007) 83-5. Trans.

^{xvi} *The village in question is Riom-ès-montagnes in the Auvergne.*

^{xvii} *Bataille and his mother "abandoned" his father in Reims not in a city or town beginning with the letter N. For biographical details, see Stuart Kendall,* Georges Bataille, *13-21.* Trans.

^{xviii} *See* Story of the Eye, *93 ff.* Trans.

^{xix} *In the notebook, this section is titled "my crack."*

^{xx} *Manuscript:*

To write is to research chance, not by an author in isolation, but by an all-becoming anonymous. In myself this carried away movement that obligates me to write is (*crossed out*: taken, carried away) in a trajectory of chance belonging to man in general. However, of chance I cannot say: "it belongs" (at each moment it can slip away); nor exactly: "I seek it": I can be it not seek it. Human chance is living trajectory, already found, but it would cease to be if

^{xxi} *Here inserted in the notebook:*

Measure (*or* Menace? *illegible* — *crossed out:* Cry) trembling for lost chance, expressing it, is for us only a blind projection taken in the movement of human chance. Neither silliness nor weakness but the state of grace.

[131]

Trembling, its (trace? *illegible*) it seemed, forever lost, the movement of chance animated my anguish.

These notes follow in the manuscript:

a) Manuscript pgs. 6-11:

In matters of sensuality, the only obstacle: the consideration of the time to come. This consideration aside, the clothes fall and, to go more quickly, the stomach relaxes. Intestinal occlusion limits the individual, without it he could not be isolated in space and in time. In erotic fury, there is no time to come, it's finished, no more dignity: I annihilate the dignity of my neighbour, my own also. All power exorbitant, it is the All-Powerful in person but in a moment of lightning, it loses its power: then he remains wrinkled, sick, soiled. Useless to hide this end. One only avoids it by skewing, going slowly, wanting to cut to wakefulness in vomit (I am not talking about death). The question of money is on the same level: no more does one want to wake up ruined. However, wanting to avoid ruin and vomit, eroticism is veiled. The summit above a chasm feels like a plain.

In matters of eroticism, time takes two forms. The desire for salvation with its counterpart, the fear of punishment. And the other part, the concern for time to come here-below. The one and the other have the same meaning: absolute in the first case, relative in the second. It is always a question of fear linked to the feeling of the duration of an identical being (isolated in space). The project in the time of an individual being is a star changed into shadows, weaving the spider's web that it becomes.

From two things one: to remain naïve and, in regard to eroticism, "to know" nothing (in this case: "being lived" by it, attaining an ultimate state without anything to premeditate — thus the unreflective but curious girl) or to reject innocence. In this last case, unquenchable thirst, each time the need to reach the summits, sense carried from excess to excess, from horror to horror. One comes to people who eat hot shit, to the characters of the *120 Days*, to the desire for desire, to these impossible people (tortures, Sade's howls, burning drool). The first path alone is happy but from the abandonment of the "project" one is on the second. Innocence assumes a "concern for time to come." "Concern" comes to failure, comes to thirst and the search. Every "project" is abandoned, the wise girl is intoxicated, pisses on herself, shows her arse. The abandonment of the "project" is the volcano, dizziness, the earth moving, drunkenness, the exorbitant sun.

[Cure for neurosis
The dream that society no longer touches anything in the depths of the being, that one touches individually. This is what the sovereignty of the "little one" means (no more sovereignty in society)
The necessity of feeling the depth to the point of feeling everything lost
Then the past, the future
The struggle of the "little one" involves man in the depths of himself]

Human knowledge in search of origins! ... Driven to betray its futility. Without stopping myself, I go further and represent, opposed to the present complexity, a simple state of things, a golden age into which the "concern for the time to come" does not enter: complete presence and consummation of lives in an erotic fire. Drunk young women and young men mixed, lost, chaos of cocks and cunts, drooling teeth that tear, hearts beating so strongly that you think you'll die. No concern of one for another, but running into death, voluptuous, simple and without comment.

Sade's weakness was having admitted a "concern for time to come": he did not live the consequences of "concern": corroding then freezing erotic life. "Concern" condemns: refusing to condemn but not knowing how to dismiss "concern," Sade invented monsters in whom "concern" and fury were mixed:
  The Président de Curval:
  "... almost sixty years of age, and worn by debauchery to a singular degree, he offered the eye not much more than a skeleton. He was tall, he was dry, thin, had two blue lustreless eyes, a livid and unwholesome mouth, a prominent chin, a long nose. Hairy as a satyr, flat-backed, with slack, drooping buttocks that rather resembled a pair of dirty rags flapping upon his upper thighs; the skin of those buttocks was, thanks to whipstrokes, so deadened and toughened that you could seize up a handful and knead it without his feeling a thing. In the centre of it all there was displayed — no need to spread those cheeks — an immense orifice whose enormous diameter, odour, and colour bore a closer

resemblance to the depths of a well-freighted privy than to an arsehole; and, crowning touch to these allurements, there was numbered among this sodomizing pig's little idiosyncrasies that of always leaving this particular part of himself in such a state of uncleanliness that one was at all times able to observe there a rim or pad a good too inches thick. Below a belly as wrinkled as it was livid and gummy, one perceived, within a forest of hairs, a tool which, in its erectile condition, might have been about eight inches long and seven around; but this condition had come to be most rare and to procure it a furious sequence of things was the necessary preliminary... Few mortals had been as free in their behavior or as debauched as the Président; but, entirely jaded, absolutely besotted, all that remained to him was the depravation and lewd profligacy of libertinage. Above three hours of excess, and of the most outrageous excess, were needed before one could hope to inspire a voluptuous reaction in him. As for his emission, although in Curval the phenomenon was far more frequent than erection, and could be observed once every day, it was, all the same, so difficult to obtain, or it never occurred save as an aftermath to things so strange and often so cruel or so unclean, that the agents of his pleasures not uncommonly often gave up, and that would give birth in him to a kind of lubricious anger that sometimes through its effects, would succeed better than their efforts." [Marquis de Sade, *120 Days of Sodom and Other Writings*, pgs. 205-6]

The impasse in which eroticism is driven back. The impossibility is not only concern for time to come. The heroes of the 120 Days are still miserable in that they cannot make the whole globe a Chateau de... This is not a hasty affirmation, but fundamentally. The impossibility in which Blangis, the Bishop, Curval find themselves is only the transposition of that in which Sade exhausted himself. Even the omnipotence of the writer, displacing at his liking the limits of the real, is itself limited, facing the possible. This amounts to saying that desire is insatiable — Sade knew it. Eroticism is an experience in which one has initial and quick triumphs. For a time, one goes from passion to passion, chance aiding the strength of the passion to accumulate, but in the end one finds its limits. Real eroticism is surpassed by desire, but desire is itself held to imagine only what is possible: the infinite passion is nonsense.

[*In margin:* the golden age is infinite passion but real eroticism leaves the golden age to enter into chance]

Nonsense thus enters into eroticism, as its necessary horizon. X. is thirty years old, but already, according to what he tells me, he seems to me to have become miserable (and resigned to himself to it). It is not that the possibilities are defective, but he dreams of an erotic society, of a human order in service to desire, constantly overheated then satisfied. This is the obsession with the golden age common to

b) Manuscript pgs 14-18:

displacement, not longer in the city, but in nature, therefore means of transportation

general loss of consciousness of a glorious destiny. expenditure as real but less tangible. Predominance of rest, softness, comfort, hospitals, and discomfort: crises, etc.

The crisis   counterpart?= neurosis

The assessment is in sum

comfort accumulated

loss of consciousness of the glorious strength of man

inviolability of economic activity

the inviolability of transcribing more clearly in religious terms the counterpart then

individualization, State, science

neurosis — love (empty beings), poetry (language), nature

In laughter, suppression of the time to come from the fact of a transference

So short a book cannot lead you where you are going. Do you doubt that this is negligible? Each being needs the absence of a solution. Naturally the book demands to be dominated from on high: the author dominates it in this way, at least he believed he did because he was not lacking in nonchalance — or in firmness. Exert yourself before the mirror. Read aloud in front of a mirror. Don't be too anguished. It won't do you any harm. Shortly you will no longer see a terrible face but rather an undecipherable expression.

One day the author saw a young man sitting on a garden bench, saying to some old men: "... evil cannot exist by itself, only as a nucleus or core. It could be that life radiates around a core of evil; the so-called sages [don't see? deny? *Illegible*] that without this core they would not have the light of colours, the chain of forces, endurance, the sacrifices that reassure them. At my age (the young man was aware of this defect) one is hardly tempted to reassure, but if I want evil, if I, even for a moment, turned my back on the good, it is to attain rigor, I felt that my virile temperament depended upon it. I habituated myself to the effort, I preferred naïveté to a boring, obscure life, without seeking to know, it sufficed for me to bear it. This seem to me to be a way to participate in the joyous enthusiasm of animals, in the ingenuity of men of other times who had only glory in mind..." The people standing before him were old professors. With the exception of one of them, almost a madman, who went along with the author, saying to him: "What is lost, and by which punishment is already hanging over its head, is speech." The madman added nothing, consistent with his argument. (His features gave off a kind of torpor, one could not know from whence his anguish came, the habitual trembling of his lips gave the impression of futility, of impotence.) The author responded politely, hiding a feeling of being overpowered: it was there as if a great number of animal-enigmas were threatening him at the same time, the old men, the madman, the young man, the grey sky, the garden trees, what could he do if not fold his back under the weight of the centuries. Agitation pursued him without ever leading him to a way out, rather each day to a new afternoon, this one grey, others sunny. How the author would have loved the young man if he had described with minute detail a position in which one could grasp the ungraspable, in which one could still speak, in which one could not speak forever, but in which — like the Archbishop of Paris who when he walked with a mistress in his gardens had three men with rakes following to erase their footprints — we are obliged to dissolve into silence a sentence scarcely formed. But the author cannot bear that the young man made a political speech to the old men.

If the young man had looked in a mirror while speaking, he would have been appropriate to his weakness. He failed to become undecipherable, not that it is good to be obscure, to express oneself poorly or keep silent: one must still make words transparent, efface a face as quickly as does a mirror, which, the instant before, was its limited gravity.

Evil cannot be the servant of the good. Freedom cannot be the good: what would freedom be without it? The object is like the unknowable, it exists one moment, a flash of a bird passing, across the heart, but that the arrow had the smallest distance, this is only the grimacing gesticulation, floods of controlled speech. Besides, the instant once passed, had the bird been reached, everything falls into the same stupor, into the same grimace.

When the infinite instant presents itself, it is good to dispose of considerable strength, to be tensed in advance. The least question being at that moment superfluous, has from now on a suspect character. A favourable interrogation nevertheless exists.

> the most venerated institutions around evil and belonging to it
> > the church and the crucifixion
> but one cannot simply say
> not sure that this will last
> in this case it would be the individuals

Georges Bataille, Romans et Récits *also includes these additional passages related to* The Little One *(369-71).*

["To Live the Impossible"]

[*Version from Notebook 5*]

In the domain of the "depths," introducing unbearable concepts [*words crossed out*] the boldest that can be formed, not to [*crossed out*] holding on, on the contrary so as to demonstrate its fragility through an equivalence of the most foolish and the most wise, the unreasonable concepts having the advantage of disturbing thought from the first blow.

In the domain of the "depths," only introducing the disturbing, the perversion of thoughts, an active and incessant destruction. Thus I can at any moment fall back on anything whatsoever, if I see the open horizon, if I lose myself in a dizzying trance, I can conclude that nothing holds; the instant thereafter the horizon closes. [But...?] each time I must respond to the unchanging interrogation in myself with different types of boldness, without a share of instability as a unique means of being at the level of the world (enduring or surmounting) nothing remains tolerable.

Imagine that through a continual excess of life or thought, one maintains between self and the world such a great ambiguity, it immediately seems that it demands a strength lacking for the most part, wherein platitude, blinders, the life of shadows lights runs to the shelter of the groove. Decline: when the groove and not harassing ambiguity is regarded as holy. (This is the slope where holiness slips senselessly, letting it be seen in the end [*two words illegible*] holiness forever the ingénue of the orgy, but, inassimilable, [blissful *or* rotting?] or killing those who approach, who have no other rest in a comic collapse.) The impossible is everywhere, demanding a derangement without measure ever always obtaining that of men considered as a group. To become the absurdity of all human discordances oneself, decline [expiration?] of horror. Elsewhere my possible is already discernable: it is "to live the impossible."

Whatever it is and in all senses, human existence is comparable to an express train full of travellers spearing the dead mechanic. The catastrophe is more or less diffuse: the impossible, horror is irremediable.

The natural reaction is to imagine a world from which catastrophes would be banished (at least invisible). At the exits from train stations and ports one could read: the impossible is forbidden to enter. Millions and millions of men have decided once and for all — even for the impossible — finally to eliminate every impossibility. The responsibility of man on earth is, it seems to them, to consecrate his time to this work of elimination: to create a possible world and not this one. They even feel their task inscribed in nature: it responds to the demands of nature, falsified by the vices and meanness of man. Thus alcohol and misery introduce into the home, gaunt children, women beaten to death. In nature, animals aren't intoxicated, life is healthy, responds to the necessities of beings. What else is there to say? It is true that even the development of possibilities introduces new impossibilities, that it is necessary to struggle to re-establish the possible, the simple viability of life. In every case man acts, the act in the sense of the possible and nothing else is conceivable. I said: in each possible one always sees a maximum of the impossible. But initially the possible must be it: it must eat, be healthy, vigorous, dispose of numerous resources, then go to the limit of the impossible, but only thereafter.

Death essentially incarnates the irremediable. The impossible is everywhere but death is indisputable. Only the most stupid imagine that science [*text breaks off*]

Two conceptions of life exist in contradiction in man.

The possible, the satisfying situation.

The impossible, putting everything in question, suppressing the sensation of viability.

The first expresses itself in the idea of God mediation.

The second in the cry God remains dead. In the first case the viability is received, in the other everything is lacking, one cries out from nothing.

Two ways to abandon the idea of God.

The first, in the sense of the possible, in a profound confidence with regard to nature, consecrating one's life to the suppression of the possible, seeing [believing ?] nothing else.

The second in the sense of the impossible, perceiving the impossible in a world without God, knowing the impossible to be immobile and the depth of things. To create a (human) possible equal to the impossible.

[*II. Version from Manuscript 2*]

Going to the depth of being, introducing untenable concepts, the boldest that one can formulate, not to hold onto them, on the contrary, in the end to mark the fragility, through an equivalence of the most senseless and the most wise, the most mad having the advantage of disturbing the most quickly.

Going to the depth of being, is not only to enter into derangement, into the perversion of thoughts, through an active and incessant destruction.

[*Crossed out*: Thus I cannot rest for even an instant (whatever that means) before the lost open horizon in dizzying trances, I cannot draw consequences from it, the horizon closes quickly.] [*A crossed out sentence legible only with difficulty.*] But one must respond to the immovable interrogation in myself each time with different types of boldness, without a share of that delirious instability — unique means of not sinking — nothing would be tolerable.

Imagining that by a continual excess of life or of thought, one maintains between oneself and the world so great an ambiguity, it immediately appears to demand a strength for the most part lacking, where platitude, blinders, the life of larva runs to the groove, to shelter. Decline: when the groove and not ambiguity is regarded as holy (this is the slope where holiness slips senselessly, letting be seen in the end, in a gripping desolation, holiness forever the ingénue of the orgy, but inassimilable, rotting those who approach). The impossible is there, demanding a derangement without measure — ever always obtaining that of the group of men. To become oneself an effect of all discordances, not annulling [*crossed out*: lacerating to the summit of laceration].

The Tomb of Louis XXX

Georges Bataille, "La Tombe de Louis XXX" in Bataille, OC IV: 151-168.

Written prior to 1947 from unused poems written between 1942 and 1945, the file contains:
1. The manuscript, accompanied by three groups of poems including "Douleur et 4 poèmes" (Pain and 4 Poems) [see OC IV: 11-13] and drafts for poems included in The Little One.
2. Three typed copies: the third copy, corrected (the text that appears in OC IV, our text) bears annotations from the printer (indicating for example a printing of 100 copies) and is itself accompanied by versions of the final page. However it seems that this projected printing did not take place: no trace of it has come to light.

The title was to have been preceded by a false title, The Tomb, *and a frontispiece:*
Manuscript: frontispiece by [Hans] Bellmer.
Note from the printer: copperplate engraving by A.M. lost.

[xxii] *In the manuscript (on a piece of calendar paper containing drafts and notes for* The Little One, The Oresteia, *"Tomb of the Wind"), this poem is entitled "Gentle-Bitterness."*

[140]

xxiii See Marquis De Sade, The 120 Days of Sodom and Other Writings, ed. & trans. Austryn Wainhouse & Richard Seaver (Grove Press, 1966) 390 ff.

In Bataille's manuscript, this other version:

The Whore: [...] one day — crowned with roses — God shat in her mouth.

xxiv In the manuscript, this other version:

> *The Stone:*
> She was so beautiful
> Herr Priest
> when God
> the father
> did it in her mouth
>
> in tears
> and naked
> laughing
> in a pink toga
>
> now here is
> a dying whore
> saying
> "To the sewer
> [...]"

This related poem, in a notebook from 1943:

Three Dead Men

Agonizing
Haloed fetid heart
Toothless woman
Rags of sadness, dirty bed
Past times
Naked, decorated with roses
In the mouth of the beauty
God relieved himself.

[141]

xxv In Bataille's Madame Edwarda *(1941), the title character shows her vagina to the narrator saying, "You can see for yourself… I am GOD." See Georges Bataille,* My Mother, Madame Edwarda, The Dead Man, *trans. by Austryn Wainhouse (Marion Boyars, 1989) 150.*

xxvi This poem is one stanza from another poem, "Je mets mon vit…" (I put my cock…) [OC IV: 14] *found among the manuscripts for* L'Archangélique [OC III: 71-96]. *Completed between August and December 1943,* L'Archangélique *was published by Editions Messages in 1944. Here Bataille's manuscript indicates the insertion of a photograph of a vulva. I have substituted Gustave Courbet's* L'Origine du Monde *(The Origin of the World, 1866), a painting Bataille would have seen at the home of its long-time owner, Jacques Lacan, second husband of Bataille's ex-wife, Sylvia Malklès.*

xxvii In the manuscript, this passage continues:

I am speaking to *you*: "Perhaps you would have loved it if I died… I do not ask you to wish it, but I am dying, can you love my death?"

And how *without reason* we must be recognizing who we cause to suffer, who we lead by the hand where we dare not go.

xxviii In the manuscript, this passage continues:

The way I myself see things: the sky, infinity, the constellations, hidden face, the rear depths, high and low, my room, my pen, and the dizziness of my breathing… As if I was myself some obtuse sphinx

    colic

tortured

    equal

        As I see the cock in a tomb, I mean the cunt of   , this is in her eyes the perfect bursting of good sense.

www.ingramcontent.com/pod-product-compliance
Lightning Source LLC
Chambersburg PA
CBHW071927130726
47909CB00014B/2601